Fin Destiny

A Rescue Alaska Mystery

by

Kathi Daley

This book is a work of fiction. Names, characters, places, and incidents either are products of the author's imagination or are used fictitiously. Any resemblance to actual events or locales or persons, living or dead, is entirely coincidental.

Copyright © 2024 by Katherine Daley

Version 1.0

All rights reserved, including the right of reproduction in whole or in part in any form.

Chapter 1

The heavy clouds littered the dark sky, moving past the nearly full moon as a flock of crows cawed in the distance. Rodents scurried through the tall grass covering the long-forgotten graves as she waited for the curse to play out. She looked toward the heavens and wondered if, after so many years of waiting, tonight would be the night. She didn't know the precise hour that she'd be called upon to do her part, but she did know that as the long days of summer melted into the crisp days of autumn, he'd finally make his way back to the place where it all began. She was sorry that his time had come and she was sorry for the role she'd play. She was sorry that despite the light he'd brought to her life, the curse had determined that, in the end, she would be the hunter, and he would be the prey.

Waking with a start, I sat up in bed, sweat covering my body. I tried to focus my eyes in the dark room, but storm clouds outside my window covered the moon, suffocating even the slightest amount of light.

"Harmony?"

"It's okay. I'm okay," I replied as my dog, Honey, jumped onto the bed and lay next to me.

"The same dream?" he asked.

"It is the same, but I'm not sure it's a dream." I allowed the rustling of dogs and cats as they stirred and then resettled to provide an anchor on which to focus my unsettled mind.

He sat up, leaned over, and wrapped his arms around me. "Do you think it was a vision rather than a dream?"

"I'm not sure." I thought back to the script that played itself out in my mind. "During my dream state, I can feel the pain this woman is experiencing as if it were my own. I experience her regret and her sorrow. She has a job to do. A destiny to fulfill. But she's sorry for the part she must play."

Houston kissed my shoulder where it met the curve of my neck and then gently pulled us back down into the softness of the mattress. "Whether a dream or vision, it's over now. You're safe here with me."

"I know," I said, burrowing down under the pile of blankets. Allowing myself to relax, I tucked my body into Houston's, taking comfort in the warmth of his embrace. Closing my eyes again, I focused on the rhythmic inhales and exhales of Honey's breath as I laid my arm over her warm body. Now that I felt secure, I tried to recall the content of my dream. I remembered a woman standing on a wooden deck in front of a wooden building, waiting for someone to arrive. I could sense this woman's pain. It was searing and intense as if it were my own. She hadn't been afraid of what was to come, but she was sorry. She had a job to do. A destiny to fulfill.

Destiny to fulfill. I rolled the concept around in my mind for a few minutes. Somehow, the word destiny didn't seem right in the context of killing someone you seemed to care about. Perhaps my interpretation of what this woman was feeling was skewed by my life experiences.

"I hate to see you go through this night after night. I wish there was a way for you to find peace," he whispered in the darkness.

"When I've had repeat dreams or visions in the past, there has always been something I needed to do."

"Do?" he asked.

"In this case, I'm not sure what I'm supposed to do, but if history is any indication, I'll likely continue to have the dreams until I figure it out."

Houston shifted a bit as his search-and-rescue dog, Kojak, jumped onto the bed and settled next to him. He ordered Kojak to lay still, which he did once he'd settled. Five of my seven dogs were sleeping in various places on the floor and on the furniture in the small bedroom we all shared. I wasn't sure what had happened to the cats. "I think we're going to need a bigger bed," Houston whispered as the two of us cozied in between Kojak, who was lying on the far-right side of the bed, Honey, who was lying on the far left, and Denali, my super protective wolf hybrid, who'd jumped up onto the bed and settled in near our feet.

"A bigger bed might be a good idea," I said with contentment. "But, at this moment, I'm pretty happy with the crowded bed."

"Do you think you'll be able to get back to sleep?" Houston asked.

"I think so," I said as I tightened my grip on Honey and allowed the tension in my body to fade away.

Chapter 2

By the time I finally clawed my way back to my life from the deep sleep I'd settled into, Houston was gone. He'd left a note on the bedside table that assured me that he'd already let the dogs out for their morning bathroom break and that he had fed all the dogs and cats, so I should sleep in for as long as my body needed rest. I smiled as I read the note. After the restless night I'd had, I was tempted to roll over and go back to sleep, but I still needed to take the dogs for a long walk and then take care of the animals in the barn before I met with my friend, Harley Medford, to discuss the special movie event he was planning for Halloween weekend.

"Twenty minutes," I said to the dogs as I put the coffee on to brew and wandered back into the bedroom to get dressed. Once I drank my coffee, I bundled up against the morning chill, grabbed my rifle, and headed out with the dogs for our regular trek to the lake and back. I'd been noticing a lot of bear activity as of late. In general, it was to be expected for an elevated level of animal activity to occur in the fall as those who hibernated packed on the pounds for the long winter ahead.

"Stay close," I instructed my husky mix, Shia. Of all the dogs in my pack, she was the most likely to wander off if I didn't keep a close eye on her. My old and partially disabled dogs, Lucky, Kodi, and Juno, tended to hobble along at a slower pace, so it wasn't uncommon for me to remind the others to hold up a bit every now and then. Denali knew he was in charge, and as such, he liked to walk in front of the pack, but he always stayed close enough to keep an eye on me, which helped with the others who tended to fall in behind him.

Once we reached the lake, I sat on a rock and waited for my younger dogs to splash around while Lucky, Juno, and Kodi rested up for the walk home. While the overnight temperatures had dipped close to freezing, now that the sun was high in the sky, the temperature had risen a good forty degrees, and I could tell that it was going to turn out to be a very nice day.

While I waited for the dogs, I decided to pull my cell phone out of my pocket and check my calendar and messages. Harley had texted to remind me of the lunch we'd scheduled later that day. Although Harley was a native Alaskan, he'd lived in Los Angeles for most of his life and had built an incredible career as a

Hollywood action star. It had been years since I'd seen him, but we'd run into each other when he'd returned home for his sister's wedding a few years ago. We'd spent some time together catching up, and the next thing I knew, Harley was buying a second home here in Rescue. While Harley lived a glamorous life in LA, he was just one of the guys when he was in Alaska. Not only did Harley actively participate in community events, but he donated money as well as his time. He really was one of the best humans I'd ever met. We'd decided to meet for lunch today to discuss the Halloween fundraiser for the local animal shelter I'd established and Harley had financed.

After lunch with Harley, I was scheduled to work a shift at Neverland, the bar and grill my best friend and brother-in-law, Jake Cartwright, owned and operated. Jake was also the head of the local search-and-rescue squad, so the bar was also used as the headquarters for the search-and-rescue team. Jake had texted to let me know there would be a team meeting at four o'clock. That worked out fine since I was scheduled to be there anyway, and Harley and I should have finished our lunch by then.

By the time the dogs and I returned from our walk, it was getting late. I still needed to shower and dress for work, so I checked the water bowls for all my inside pets, and then Honey and I headed to the barn where my blind mule, Homer, lived with the rabbits I'd rescued from time to time.

"How's everyone doing today?" I asked the animals as I began cleaning pens. Honey wandered over to say hi to Homer, who I fed first. "I guess you've noticed that Kodi and Juno have moved over to the house," I told the mule. "It took some persuasion on my part since they both prefer to sleep in the barn, but given their age and worsening arthritis, I felt that it was better for them to be indoors now that the temperatures are dropping so low at night."

I wasn't sure whether Homer cared about the dogs one way or the other, but they had been roommates for lots of years, so I felt I should explain their absence.

I continued to talk as I worked. It wasn't that I thought the animals could actually understand what I was saying, but in my opinion, hearing my voice was a comfort to them. Once I'd finished in the barn, I called Honey, and we headed inside so that I could shower and dress for the day.

Chapter 3

Harley and his dog, Brando, lived in an enormous house on a large plot of land with a private lake. I knew Brando would enjoy some doggy company, so I decided to bring my search-and-rescue dog, Yukon, with me. Brando and Yukon were close in age, and each enjoyed the company of the other. We were having a search-and-rescue meeting at Neverland later in the day, so it seemed appropriate to bring Yukon along for that as well. During my shift at the bar, I figured Yukon could hang out with Gunther, the old dog my good friend, Sarge, was fostering.

"Oh good, you brought someone for Brando to hang out with," Harley said after hugging me hello and then greeting Yukon. "Brando gets so much attention when he is on a shoot with me that I think it takes him some time to get used to the slower pace of life here in Alaska."

"I can understand that. And I'm happy to hear that Brando is doing so well on the movie sets. I know you've struggled with the decision of whether to take him with you or leave him here with me."

"Brando loves hanging out with you and your pack, but he's a very social dog who loves all the hustle and bustle of being on location."

I smiled. "I'm happy to hear that. When you first agreed to adopt Brando, I could see that you were unsure of things, but everything seems to have worked out wonderfully."

Harley glanced at his best buddy as he ran around his backyard with Yukon. "He is the perfect companion for me." He glanced at me. "Speaking of perfect companions, I just found out this morning that my friend, Ava, plans to visit Alaska over Halloween."

"Ava Arlington?"

Ava Arlington was both a singer and an actress, and I knew that she'd recently costarred in a movie Harley had filmed on location in Australia.

He nodded. "We were chatting on the phone the other day, and she mentioned having an idea for a thriller set in Alaska. She wanted to pick my brain, and while I was more than happy to answer all her questions, I suggested that if she wanted to get a feel for the place, she should come and visit. She's currently filming a movie in Canada and won't be free until around mid-October, so I suggested she come when she could and stay through Halloween. She called this morning to let me know she plans to arrive on the twentieth."

"That's awesome. I can't wait to meet her."

"I told her all about you, and she's excited to meet you as well. I also told her about our shelter and the Halloween fundraiser we're planning, and she suggested a *Rocky Horror Picture Show* sing-along."

"Sing-along?" I asked.

Harley explained. "Basically, you show the movie, but there are actors who act out certain scenes and lead a sing-along with the audience for all the musical numbers."

"And Ava is willing to be one of these actors?"

"She is. If she and I take on the main roles, we won't need anyone else to learn a lot of lines, although we will need a couple of local actors to fill some of the minor roles. I know others who have done this as a fundraiser, and they've earned a lot of money. Of course, we'll need to get started on it right away. Halloween is less than two months away."

I jumped up and hugged Harley. "Ava Arlington is going to put on a show in our little theater. This is going to be huge."

"It is going to be huge," Harley agreed, hugging me back. "If we really want to cash in on this, we'll need a larger space than the local theater."

"Larger space? I'm not sure we have a larger space."

"I thought that one of the empty warehouses near the shelter would be perfect. We can build a stage and hang a screen."

"How are we ever going to find enough chairs to fill a warehouse?"

"We'll promote the event as a BYOC."

"Bring your own chair," I said.

He nodded. "We'll need to set up some rules about the size of the chair each ticket holder can bring, but I'm sure everyone in town has a folding chair, dining room chair, or even lawn chair."

"That's brilliant." I hugged Harley again. I supposed my enthusiasm was contagious since both dogs started barking this time. "We need to nail down a date and then confirm that there's a warehouse available to rent. We'll also need to look into logistics such as heat. I think this could work, and with you and Ava Arlington both on the stage, I'm sure we'll earn enough with this one fundraiser to take care of the shelter's expenses for the next year."

Before Harley moved to town, finding enough cash to open even a small local shelter had been a struggle. Once Harley and his celebrity friends became involved, not only did we suddenly have funds for expenses but for expansion and training as well.

"We need to start making notes," I said.

"I agree, but I made a reservation with Chloe for lunch, so perhaps we should head out and talk on the way." Harley referred to my best friend, Chloe Rivers, who owned and operated a local diner.

"That sounds good. It's been a while since I've gotten together with Chloe. Does she know about the idea you have for the fundraiser?"

"I wanted to run it past you before I mentioned it to anyone else." He picked up his tablet, which had been charging on his kitchen counter. "Since you're onboard with the idea, we can begin planning while we eat."

"Sounds good to me," I said as my cell phone rang. "It's Serena," I said, glancing at the caller ID. "I should get this." I referred to Rescue Animal Shelter's full-time employee, Serena Walters.

I could feel Harley watching my face as I listened to what Serena had to say. A hiker had come into the shelter to report a baby moose sighting. He said he watched the baby from a distance for a while and didn't notice the mother nearby. The man admitted that he didn't know a lot about the wildlife in the area and was concerned about disturbing the moose and didn't want to accidentally "rescue" a moose who didn't require rescuing, so he simply pinned the location of the baby moose onto the map program on his cell phone and then stopped by the shelter to report it on his way home. I was glad that the man hadn't attempted his own moose rescue. Well-meaning hikers and hunters often made things worse when they tried to help the local wildlife. The truth of the matter was that moose mamas sometimes left their babies for short periods, but that didn't mean they had abandoned them.

"I need to go and check this out," I said to Harley. "I'm sorry about our lunch."

"This is more important. I'll go with you. You might need help."

"I'd appreciate that. We should leave the dogs here so they don't get in the way, and I'll need to stop by the shelter to get the supplies I'll need if the baby appears to be injured, and it looks like the best course of action is to bring him in. Your truck has a lot more room than my Jeep, so if you don't mind getting it dirty, perhaps you should drive."

"I'd be happy to. How far do we need to travel?"

I looked at the pin Serena had forwarded to me. "I'd say it will take about a half hour to get to the location where the baby moose was last seen. Honestly, there's a good chance the mama will have returned by now, but it never hurts to check it out."

While most calls relating to abandoned moose babies turned out to be false alarms, we did occasionally find that the mama had died and the calf actually did require an intervention. When a calf was actually orphaned, we'd temporarily bring them to the shelter until the appropriate rescue group could be notified.

"What happened to the baby moose you fostered a few years ago?" Harley asked after we'd gathered the equipment we needed and headed north. "If I recall correctly, his name was Rocky. I remember he was moved to a rescue specializing in orphaned calves, but I left the area to do a movie and never did hear what happened to him."

"Rocky is doing great. He initially went to a rescue but has been released back into the wild, and he's doing very well at this point."

"So you're tracking him?"

"We are. By tracking the animals we rehabilitate and release, we're able to gather data that helps us make better decisions as we move forward. You're going to take a left onto that dirt road about a half mile up."

Harley slowed and made the turn. He decreased his speed even more once we started down the rutted dirt road. "I remember that Honey sort of adopted the baby."

"She did. Honey is a natural-born mama. She was already pregnant when she was found, so she had one litter and seemed to be in her element. I was nervous about having her spayed, but it was the right thing to do. Since then, she's fostered kittens, the moose, puppies who have been separated from their mama at a young age, a bear cub, and even a baby rabbit I found in a trap."

"If the moose calf has been abandoned, will you take him home or to the shelter?" Harley wondered.

"I don't know if we have an empty pen at the shelter. If we do, I may leave the calf with Serena, but if we don't, I'll take him home until other arrangements can be made. When my barn was rebuilt, we designed a pen with abandoned wildlife in mind, so I have a place to keep him." I glanced at my cell phone. "You're going to see a narrow trail on the right. I'd say it's a few hundred yards ahead. Once we get to the trail, we'll park and continue on foot."

Once we abandoned the truck and set off on foot, all conversation came to an end. If the little guy was still in the area, we didn't want to scare him. Personally, I hoped that his mama had come for him and he was long gone by this point, but I knew that if I didn't personally take the time to check it out, I'd always wonder if the baby actually was abandoned or just waiting for his mama to return from her walkabout.

We paused and crouched down as we approached the meadow where the hiker had seen the calf. Trees were lining the meadow's perimeter, so we decided to pause behind a grove featuring thick underbrush. Once we were settled, we scanned the area using our binoculars.

"I don't see him," Harley whispered.

"Yeah, I don't either. The grass is pretty tall, so if the calf's lying down, it may be hard to see him. Let's watch for a while and see if we notice any movement. If the little guy is napping, we may not see him unless he stands up."

Harley put the binoculars he'd brought up to his eyes. He made a few adjustments before scanning the entire area. "Check out that shady area near the rocks on the far left of us. It looks like there might be something there."

I put my binoculars up to my eyes and looked toward the shady area where Harley was looking. It did look as if there might be something lying in the grass.

"It seems to me that a mama moose would keep her baby close by at all times," Harley said. "By being on his own out here, he's susceptible to predators."

"I don't disagree with the thought, but I've come across too many calves out on their own only to have the mama return for them after a while to not at least consider that mama has simply stepped away for a few minutes."

"How long has it been since the hiker saw the calf?"

"About three hours," I answered. I considered the landscape around us. "Maybe we can slowly make our way around the perimeter of the meadow and get a closer look at that shady area. If the calf is simply napping, my intuition is that his mama might very well be nearby. When a calf has actually been abandoned, they'll usually wander around, calling for their mama. The fact that this one appears to have settled in for a nap seems to indicate that he might know that his mama is nearby."

"Maybe the calf has been abandoned but is simply too tired to wander around and cry," Harley suggested.

"Maybe. Let's head around the perimeter in a counterclockwise direction. Keep your eyes open as we walk." I gripped the rifle I held. "We'll need to watch for the mama and any predators who might have latched onto his scent."

Harley and I moved slowly, stopping to look around as we walked. There were footprints in the mud, which had been left by both an adult moose and a baby moose, indicating that the mama had been here at one point. We were about halfway between the spot where we started and the shady area we were heading toward when we saw the calf pop up. He looked around but didn't seem to be in a panic. We continued watching for a few minutes while he simply stood there looking around.

"There's something in the brush just behind the calf," Harley whispered. "I can see tree branches moving, and I hear rustling caused by someone or something moving through them."

I hoped it was the mama and not a predator. The last thing I wanted to do was to have to decide whether or not a grizzly was entitled to the meal he needed to survive.

"It's the cow," Harley said.

I blew out a breath of relief as the baby trotted over to his mama.

"Do you think she's been in the area this entire time?"

I shrugged. "I'm not sure where the mama's been, but I know that calves are sometimes left alone to wait for their mama to return. We constantly tell hikers who come across calves who appear abandoned to wait and watch. If the cow hadn't shown in the next few hours, we would have had to have decided whether or not to intervene, so I'm glad she returned when she did."

Harley and I stood perfectly still as the calf and his mama reunited, watching as they headed off together in the direction from which the cow had appeared.

"I guess we should head back," I said after the mama and baby disappeared from sight. "I'm sorry we missed our lunch. I have a search-and-rescue meeting that I'm going to be very late for and then a shift at Neverland. If you want to stop by, I'll comp your meal."

"I'd like that, but I guess we should head back and get the dogs, and we should probably check in with Serena first."

"Yeah, and I need to wash up. I'll call Jake and let him know what's going on."

As it turned out, all of that took longer than I anticipated. Harley called Serena for me, and during the conversation, he ended up agreeing to meet with her to go over the budget, so he took a raincheck on his free meal, and I headed home to change my clothes. But by the time I got to Neverland, it was ten minutes after five, and the rest of the team were already there and waiting.

"Sorry, guys," I said to my team members, Jake Cartwright, Landon Stafford, Wyatt Forester, and Sarge. "I was meeting with Harley about the fundraiser for the shelter, and then I got the call about the calf a hiker reported as being abandoned. The whole thing took a lot longer than I anticipated."

"Did mama show up?" Wyatt asked.

"She did. The calf was left alone for about three hours, which, given the little guy's size, seemed odd to me, but I know that sort of situation does occur. I'm just glad the hiker left the calf alone and contacted us."

"It'd be hard to just leave a calf on his own, but I do know it's the right thing to do," Sarge said.

"Where are Dani and Jordan?" I asked about Dani Matthews, our helicopter pilot, and Jordan Fairchild, a doctor, search-and-rescue team member, and Jake's live-in girlfriend.

"Jordan is doing home visits in the rural areas this week, and Dani is flying her to the villages that don't have road access."

"I guess Jordan did mention something about that," I said. There were many wonderful things about living in the Alaskan outback, but one of the challenging things was access to health care when there was limited road access to many areas. "Are they flying home each night?"

"They are," Jake answered. "Of course, at this point, they're taking care of individuals who live off the grid but are still within a few hours flight of Rescue. I'm not sure what is going to happen once they venture out a bit."

I had to admire Jordan for doing what she was doing. She didn't have to service those individuals who couldn't make it into town for medical care, but she did it anyway. In fact, one of the first things she did after signing on with our local hospital was to establish the practice of making house calls to those living in out-of-the-way areas.

"Can we talk about my big news now?" Wyatt asked.

I could see he was clearly excited about something.

"We can," Jake said. "As you all know, I've been considering taking on another search-and-rescue dog. I spoke to the man who trained Sitka, and he agreed to locate and prepare another candidate. He called me this week to let me know that he found the perfect dog, and he's already trained and will be able to help out right away."

"That's great," everyone said at once.

I knew how essential rescue dogs were when it came to improving the odds of a successful rescue.

"Jake asked me to be his handler," Wyatt jumped in.

I smiled at my friend. "That's awesome. I'm happy for you, Wyatt."

Jake spoke. "While anyone in the group would make a wonderful handler, I already have Sitka, and Harmony already has Yukon. Wyatt just bought a house with a large fenced-in yard, and his schedule allows him to make it to most of the rescues. Wyatt will fly to Bryton Lake for some one-on-one training sessions with Timber, and then Wyatt will accompany him home."

I could tell that the group as a whole was happy for Wyatt. He'd started off with the group as sort of a goofball, and Jake rarely asked him to take on any sort of leadership role or added responsibility, but I think we could all see that he'd grown up quite a bit since he almost died during a rescue a few years ago and I had to agree with Jake that Wyatt was ready to take on more than he had in the past.

Once the congratulations had died down, Jake segued into an update on the new equipment he'd ordered, followed by the announcement of upcoming training exercises and the date and time for the next meeting. Once that was accomplished, the group broke up. Sarge headed toward the kitchen to begin the prep work for the dinner menu, Jake went into his office to return some calls, Wyatt took his place behind the bar, and I put my apron on and prepared for my shift. Landon was the only team member who'd attended the meeting who didn't work at Neverland, so he slipped onto a stool at the bar and chatted with Wyatt while he prepped the bar.

Despite the nice weather, it was slow tonight, so when Houston called to let me know he was going to be late meeting up with me, I suggested he meet me at my cabin rather than at the bar and grill since Jake had noticed my fatigue due to my lack of sleep the past few nights and was sending me home early.

Chapter 4

She sat on the low stone wall and waited for him to arrive. She remembered her anger and deeply felt desperation when her family had decided to leave their home and move to the barren mining town perched on the side of a mountain. She remembered her fear. She remembered wanting to die. But then she'd found out that he'd be there, and all at once, what had seemed like a death sentence had suddenly become the adventure of a lifetime. She owed him so much. He'd filled a void in her life and brought her joy despite the circumstances. She didn't know what the future would bring, but she was sure they'd be friends forever.

When I woke, I was in bed, and the room was pitch black. Odd, I didn't remember going to bed. In fact, the last thing I remembered was lying down on my sofa while I waited for Houston to arrive. I supposed I must have fallen asleep, and he must have carried me into the bedroom. I wondered if Houston was here and reached out a hand to find the bed next to me empty. Houston didn't always stay over, and I supposed it made sense that he'd head home once he realized I was out cold and would likely not wake until the following morning.

I leaned on my elbows and tried to focus my eyes in the darkness. The wind pounded against my tiny cabin as sheets of rain pelted my tin roof. Jake had mentioned that a storm was moving in our direction. He'd said it was a fast-moving storm that would blow in with a vengeance and was likely to have left the area by the time we woke in the morning.

I glanced at the bedside clock. Three-seventeen. Much too early to get up. Between the wind and the rain outside my cabin walls and the restless animals within those same walls, I wasn't sure if I'd be able to get back to sleep, but I knew I had to try, so I laid back down and listened to the storm. Turning onto my side, I tucked my therapy cat, Moose, into my chest. Honey repositioned herself and settled in behind me. I always felt safe with my animals. They were my lifeline in what often turned out to be a topsy-turvy world.

As I lay quietly under the multitude of blankets I had piled on my bed, I thought back to my dream. I'd experienced the event through the eyes of a child. A young girl. It was hard to say how old she was, but I felt sure she hadn't reached maturity. She had been waiting for a boy. A boy she considered to be a friend. A boy who brought light to her day during a time when her life had taken a challenging turn. It was an odd sort of dream. On the surface, it should have been a happy dream, but I could sense that what I had experienced was a sad memory. I felt that the dream I'd just experienced had either been a shared dream or a shared memory with the woman the child had become.

I rolled over and tried to find a more comfortable position. I really did want to go back to sleep, but my mind was busy. Who was this woman? Why did I keep sharing her memories? And was it a memory or merely a dream? Given the intensity of the whole thing, I supposed that I might actually be having a vision of things yet to come. A warning of sorts. Most of the time, when I had vivid dreams that reoccurred over time, there was something that I had to do. A duty I must fulfill if I wanted them to stop. In this case, I wasn't sure what that duty might be. If this was a portent of things to come, was I supposed to find this woman and stop her from doing what she clearly didn't want to do? Or was it my task to simply understand her pain?

I pulled the pile of blankets over my head and tried to remember where this woman had been standing. In the first set of dreams, an adult woman stood on a wooden deck looking out over a cemetery that appeared to have been deserted for decades. Large mountains had been beyond the cemetery. Perhaps the woman had been waiting in one of the many mining towns that had sprung up around the turn of the century, but by this point, were nothing more than ghost towns. A ghost town would explain a lot. I thought about the wooden deck the woman had been standing on in my dreams. It was old and weathered with age, as was the cemetery she was looking at.

In my most recent dream, the young girl had been sitting on a low rock wall. It was spring, and the wildflowers were blooming. The setting was a happy sort of setting as opposed to the foreboding of the first dreams.

I felt like I recognized the mountains in the background of both dreams, but I couldn't quite place them. As I continued focusing on the details, the intense emotions of the dream began to fade, and with the release of those emotions came peace and sleep.

Chapter 5

Houston showed up at my front door just as I was beginning to wake up. I rolled out of bed, pulled my heavy sweatshirt on, slipped my feet into furry slippers, and went to answer the door.

"Good morning." I smiled as I stepped aside to allow him to enter.

He held up a to-go bag. "I brought breakfast sandwiches and coffee. You fell asleep before we had the chance to eat last night, so I figured you'd be hungry."

"I am hungry," I admitted while placing two logs into the wood-burning stove. "I'm sorry I fell asleep before you arrived. You could have woken me up."

"You looked exhausted, so I figured it was best to allow you to sleep. I thought you might wake up when I carried you into your room, took off your shoes, and tucked you into bed, but you were out cold."

"It's been a tough week," I admitted. "The dreams have become a nightly ritual that leaves me feeling out of sorts."

His eyes softened as he offered me a look of support. "I hate to see you go through this night after night. Do you feel like you understand the dreams and why you might be having them?"

"Not really. The dreams are odd, and I'm not sure I have a handle on things, but the images in my mind are becoming clearer. I think I might even know where the dreams are located."

"Located?"

"In the first set of dreams, the woman is near a cemetery. I've thought about it and feel certain that the woman is waiting outside the cemetery near the abandoned mining camp on Grizzly Mountain. I wasn't sure where she was at first, but then I had another dream last night, a different dream where a young girl was waiting on a low rock wall, and suddenly the images in my mind began to make sense."

"What did you mean when you said that she was waiting?"

"Not literally," I said. "Not in real-time. I think my dream is a memory. Not my memory but hers."

"So, do you think that you're connecting with this woman as the two of you sleep?"

"I think that might be what's happening. To be honest, I can't know for sure. But the emotions felt during the dream seem to be the sort of thing that could only be experienced by the one who lived it."

Houston shifted as his dog, Kojak, positioned himself next to the table. I had a feeling he was hoping that someone would drop something, affording him a morning snack.

"So what are you suggesting?" Houston asked as I refilled both our mugs with coffee.

"I think I need to make the trip up to the cemetery. I'm beginning to form a picture of a woman who, as a child, had a friend she cared for deeply. The odd thing is, I'm fairly certain the child who was waiting with such happy anticipation for the boy to arrive in the dream I had last night is the same woman who kills the man the boy has become many years later."

Houston screwed up his face. "Well, that's depressing. Are you sure?"

"Actually, no, I'm not sure. At this point, however, that's my gut instinct. I can't say that I have all the answers, but I think I have a part to play in whatever is going on. An important part that shouldn't be ignored."

"What sort of part?"

"I'm not sure. The woman seems to want me to do something. I don't have it all figured out, but I do have this gut feeling that I need to do whatever this woman needs me to do if I am ever going to get any peace. I don't know if the dream is a memory and I simply need to understand what occurred and why it occurred, or if it's a portent, and I need to stop the adult woman from doing what she clearly plans to do."

"And you think visiting the cemetery will help?" Houston asked.

"A physical link to the place all this went down might help. I need to do something, or these dreams are going to drive me insane."

Houston took a sip of his coffee. I sensed he needed a minute to think about what I'd just said before replying. "Okay. Let's say you do need to visit the location in your dream. Where exactly is this cemetery?"

"As I said, I think the events I'm dreaming about take place near that old mining camp on Grizzly Mountain."

"That mining camp shut down sixty years ago. It's just a ghost town at this point."

"Yes. But a ghost town seems to fit the narrative."

Houston took another sip of his coffee. "Okay. I trust that you know what you need to do. When do you want to go?"

"As soon as possible. I'm pretty sure that my dreams are only going to become more intense if I don't do my part."

Houston sat back in his chair. It appeared that, once again, he was pausing to think things over.

Houston was the deliberate sort who tended to take his time making decisions. Most of the time, I appreciated that. "If you're going to head up the mountain, I'm going to come with you," he finally said. "We can go tomorrow. Things have been slow in town lately. I need to meet with my team in the morning, but we can head out after that."

"We should get an early start. It's a long drive."

"I was thinking we could drive part way tomorrow. We can stay in that little town that grew up around the old base camp settlement after the mine closed."

"Grizzly Flats," I said, voicing the name of the small town that Houston had referred to.

"Yes, Grizzly Flats. They have a small hotel there next to the post office. I'll call and make a reservation for tomorrow night. That way, we'll get a good night's sleep in the hotel, and we'll be able to head up the mountain first thing Saturday morning. Even if we start from Grizzly Flats, it'll be a long drive up to the abandoned mine, so we should bring overnight gear just in case we end up needing it. Do you have someone to take care of the animals?"

"I'll call Serena. As long as she doesn't have plans, I'm sure she'll be happy to do it. If the hotel allows dogs, we can bring Kojak and Yukon with us. You never know when a good search-and-rescue dog might come in handy."

"That sounds good to me. I'll ask about the dogs when I make the reservation."

"Speaking of dogs," I said, "during the meeting yesterday, Jake told us that we're getting another search-and-rescue dog."

"You are? That's wonderful. Will he be living with Jake?"

"With Wyatt, actually."

Houston raised a brow. "Really?"

"He just bought that new house, so he has a fenced yard, and Jake seems to think he's ready."

"He does seem to take things a bit more seriously lately. How is the renovation on the house coming along?"

"Good, I think. Sarge and Gunther have been helping him almost every day before Neverland opens."

"Sarge knows about home renovation?"

"No, not really, but he does like to help out. To tell you the truth, even though Sarge is surrounded by people all day, every day, working at Neverland, I think he's lonely. Still, despite all the company, other than me, I think that Wyatt is Sarge's favorite. Wyatt can be a bit of a goofball, but he also has a soft side. I think he's been like a son to Sarge."

"I guess I can see that." Houston took a bite of his sandwich. "One of the first things that struck me about the S&R team when I first met you was that you really cared about each other. In many ways, you're a family."

"We really are," I agreed. "And I thank God for that family every day."

The first thing I did after Houston left was call Serena to verify that she would be able to keep an eye on my pack. I hated being gone overnight and tried to stay as close to home as possible, but there were occasions when an overnight trip was necessary. I have an excellent support system, so I knew that at least one of my friends would always be willing to make sure my menagerie of animals was well taken care of on those rare occasions. While several friends had filled this need for me in the past, I figured I'd start with Serena since I'd recently spoken to her and didn't think she had plans for the weekend.

"So you and Houston are going camping?" she asked with a tone of doubt in her voice once I explained where I was going and how long I planned to be away. "It's been pretty cold at night."

"I wanted to head up to the old cemetery near the abandoned mining camp on Grizzly Mountain to check out a few things, so we decided to bring supplies along just in case we need to spend the night. Houston plans to take tomorrow afternoon off in addition to Saturday and Sunday, so I think we're just going to head to the little town at the foot of the mountain tomorrow and then spend the night at the hotel next to the post office. We'll get an early start on Saturday and head up the mountain. If all goes as planned, we should be able to get in and out in one day, but you know how things go."

"I do know how things go, and it's a long trek up there, even if you are starting from Grizzly Flats. I think you're wise to bring supplies. Houston has a camper shell on his truck, so you'll be able to get out of the elements if you need to sleep up there."

"I'm not worried about it. We're going to bring Kojak and Yukon with us, but all the other dogs will be here."

"Okay. I'm sure we'll be fine. Even Denali seems to like me at this point."

"I think the pack has adopted you as one of their own. How did your meeting with Harley go yesterday?"

"It went well. I was afraid that we were going to come up short this winter, but then Harley shared his idea for the Halloween fundraiser. I can't believe that Ava Arlington is going to participate."

"I know. I was super excited when Harley shared his idea with me."

Serena paused and then asked the question I'd half been expecting. "Harley mentioned that Ava would be staying with him. Do you think anything is going on between Ava and Harley?"

I knew that Serena had developed feelings for Harley beyond those between boss and employee, but after speaking to Harley about it, I also knew it was unlikely that her feelings would ever be reciprocated. Still, I did understand Serena's concern, so I carefully answered. "I'm pretty sure that Ava is just coming to town to do research for her movie, and Harley volunteered to play host and show her around."

"Are you sure?"

"No, I'm not sure, but Harley didn't say anything to me that would indicate that Ava was anything more than a friend."

I decided to change the subject since I knew the topic of Harley with other women was sensitive for Serena. Instead, I talked about the baby moose that Harley and I had tracked the previous day. I shared how lucky it was that the man who had first seen him had decided to leave him where he was and contact us rather than trying to help directly, and then I suggested that we might want to print educational literature to hand out that covered these sorts of things.

Once I hung up with Serena, I decided to call Jake and let him know that while I would be in today as planned, I'd need tomorrow as well as Saturday and Sunday off.

"I guess we can survive without you this weekend. Are you feeling okay?" Jake asked.

"I'm feeling fine. Houston and I are heading out of town for the weekend, and we decided to leave tomorrow."

"Really? Where are you going?"

"Grizzly Mountain."

He didn't respond. I supposed he was trying to make sense out of this.

"You know I've been having those dreams," I continued.

"The one with the woman waiting for someone in the graveyard?"

"Yes. I had the dream again last night and realized that the woman in my dreams was waiting for whoever she was waiting for at the old cemetery near the deserted mining camp on Grizzly Mountain. I felt compelled to head up there to check it out, and Houston volunteered to go with me."

"It's a long haul up there, and it recently snowed in the higher elevations," he cautioned.

"I know. Houston has to work tomorrow morning, but he's taking off at midday, and we're going to drive to Grizzly Flats and spend the night in the hotel. We'll get an early start Saturday morning and, hopefully, make it in and out in one day. We're taking Houston's big four-wheel drive truck with the camper shell and supplies to get us through should we need to spend the night, so we'll be fine even if we don't make it back tomorrow."

"And the animals?"

"We're taking Kojak and Yukon with us, and Serena is going to stay with the rest of the crew. I'm sure she'll be fine, but you know how Denali can be. It might be nice if you would check in with her to make sure she's okay."

"I can do that. Are you coming in for your shift today?"

"I'll be there."

"Okay, I'll see you then."

After I hung up with Jake, I began packing for our trip. Of course, having lived in Alaska my entire life and being well aware of all the possible obstacles that one might run into after setting out across the country, I packed a ton of outerwear, a box full of blankets, several bags of food, gallons upon gallons of water, sleeping bags, and wood and fuel for a fire. I also packed flashlights, flares, and a camp stove. If we ended up making it up to the camp without incident, as we planned to accomplish at this point, I'd need to put all the supplies away when we returned home, but life in this climate had taught me that it was better to be overprepared than underprepared.

Chapter 6

I'd just arrived at Neverland for my shift when Sarge got a call about a hiker who'd fallen off a cliff and needed to be rescued. We usually used Dani's helicopter to both rescue and transport the victim when we were tasked with these sorts of medivacs, but in this case, since Dani had taken Jordan to a remote village north of us, her bird was unavailable.

"We'll have to take the trucks," Jake said. "My truck is outfitted with the equipment we need, so Wyatt will ride with me. Harmony, you ride along with Landon." He turned and looked at Sarge. "You can run the command post from here."

"What we need is a second chopper with a pilot we can call on when Dani is unavailable," Landon said as he and I walked out to his truck.

"I definitely agree with that. We could also use a backup doctor on the team."

"A backup doctor would be a luxury, but I agree that having one would be helpful."

Once we were on the road, I asked Landon what he knew about the hiker we were going after. Since I'd literally walked in just as Jake and the others were packing to head out, I hadn't heard the entire backstory.

"Four friends were hiking Desolation Pass, and one of the four wandered over to the edge of a ledge to take a closer look at the scenery. The ledge gave way, which, in my opinion, the hiker should have anticipated due to all the rain we've had. When the ground gave way, the man fell and landed on another much narrower ledge about fifty feet below the first ledge."

Usually, we'd have the chopper lower rescue workers down to the victim, but in this case, we would most likely need to use ropes to lower rescuers down.

"At least the men were on their way back from their excursion, and the fall victim isn't too far up the mountain," I said. "Based on the coordinates Jake texted me, it looks as if we'll be able to take the trucks the entire way, which will save a lot of time."

"If the man is still alive, then the fact that he's within driving range just might make all the difference," Landon agreed.

When we arrived at the site, the three friends who had witnessed the fall were gathered in a group close to the edge but not close enough to end up on the ledge below as their friend had. Landon parked his truck next to Jake's, and then he and I joined Jake and Wyatt, who had arrived shortly before us.

"We're going to need to use ropes and send two men down with the backboard," Jake said. He looked toward the edge of the cliff face. "The edge is unstable, so we'll need to make sure that anyone who isn't tied to a rope stays well back." He looked toward Landon's truck. "Both my truck and Landon's have a winch. Wyatt and I will tie our ropes to the winch and then carefully make our way down to the victim. Harmony and Landon can work the winches and make sure the lines don't get tangled or caught on something." He looked directly at me. "To be safe, the two of you should anchor yourself with ropes as well in case you need to approach the ledge to feed the ropes down."

Everyone agreed with Jake's plan, and we got to work finding the optimal place to park the trucks and then began securing the lines. Once that was accomplished, Jake and Wyatt slowly made their way toward the cliff's edge. As Jake had anticipated, part of the ledge gave way with the men's weight, but without a chopper, going down from the top was the only way to get to the victim. In these sorts of situations, slow and steady was the best course of action, so it was a long, agonizing journey for both men as they tried to reach the victim without sending additional dirt and rocks down on him.

"We're on the ledge," Jake called up.

Landon and I stopped feeding the rope.

"He has a pulse, but he's out cold. Give Wyatt and me a few minutes to get him situated and secured on the rescue board, and then you can begin winching us all up."

The man was critically injured with multiple broken bones, so Jake and Wyatt had to take their time so as not to risk hurting him further. Once he was loaded, Landon and I would need to raise the backboard up from the ledge where the man had landed. Keeping him totally level and not getting the board and its occupant caught on any of the rocks and roots that were jutting out from the side of the cliff's face was going to be challenging.

"Okay," Jake called out. "Begin pulling him up. Slowly."

Landon and I did as Jake instructed, but even though we tried to bring the victim up slowly and steadily, an additional section of the ledge broke off and rained down on everyone below.

"Hold up," Jake called.

"Are you okay?" I could barely resist the urge to run to the edge and look over to confirm that my friends were safe.

"I'm okay. Just give us a minute to straighten the backboard."

Once Jake had righted things to the best of his ability, he instructed us to start again. Slow and steady, I reminded myself as I ran the winch on Jake's truck. There was no way we were going to get the victim, Jake, and Wyatt all up that cliff without small pieces of debris letting loose. I just hoped we could prevent any major breaks which could potentially lead to the injury or even death of all the men.

"We're about halfway up," Jake called out. "Continue to run the winches slow and steady until I tell you to stop."

"Okay," I called back, holding my breath as each agonizing minute ticked by.

Once the backboard was a few feet below the lip, Jake called out for us to stop what we were doing. He wanted to ensure that he and Wyatt were in place so they could lift the victim up and over the edge while avoiding putting too much strain on the vulnerable earth along the lip of the ledge.

Once Jake was in place, he instructed Landon and me to pull all four lines up slowly and evenly. I held my breath as Jake, Wyatt, and the backboard with the victim came into view. Once the trio was safely on solid ground, Wyatt helped Jake load the victim into his truck. Jake, who had the most medical training, second only to Jordan, who was a licensed doctor, would ride in the back with the victim while Wyatt drove his truck. Landon volunteered to assist Jake with the victim, so I took on the duty of driving Landon's truck back to town. At this point, I still didn't know if our fall victim was going to make it. He was in bad shape, and the doctor who admitted him to the clinic indicated that things weren't looking all that good.

By the time we made it back to Neverland, we were all exhausted. Jake decided to keep the bar and grill closed for the evening, but Sarge had already made a big pot of soup, so he offered it to the team, and we all happily accepted. By the time I got home, all I had strength left for was a quick shower and an early night in bed.

Chapter 7

I woke early the following morning and realized that for the first time in a long time, I hadn't shared my dreams with the woman from the cemetery. I paused to consider the implications of this but eventually decided to take advantage of my refreshed state and take the dogs for a long walk. Between the rain, which had turned to snow and then turned back to rain, and the overcast nature of the day, the walk to the lake and back was cold and dreary. Houston had called to confirm he'd be by around noon to pick me up for our trip to Grizzly Flats, and I assured him I'd be ready. I hated to leave my animals, even if it was only for a few days, so I planned to spend as much time with them as I could before we left.

With the wet ground, tracks left by those who had passed this way were even more apparent than they usually were. "Cougar," I said aloud. My cabin was located in an isolated area away from town, so it wasn't uncommon to have animals of all types stop by for a visit. Since cougars had a way of sneaking up on you. I knew I'd need to be extra vigilant as we passed through the section of the trail that was dense with trees and scattered with rock formations.

Once the trail opened up a bit, I began to relax. The large cat posed the biggest threat to my older dogs, Juno, Kodi, and Lucky. I made sure they walked right next to me. With Denali at the head of the pack, it was unlikely that a cougar, or any predator for that matter, would get to us before he went after them, but I didn't want to put my protector in the position of needing to risk his life to save ours.

Once we reached the lake, I paused to rest. Those dogs with a higher energy level ran around, and those who needed to catch their breath took a power nap, giving me time to think about the dreams I'd been having and my plan to attempt to stop them. After about thirty minutes, I called all the dogs, turned around, and began to retrace my steps. Given the situation, the woman who had been sharing my dreams for almost two weeks now had occupied my attention more than I ought to have let her, which is why I was surprised when we came around a corner and came face to face with a grizzly.

Denali began to bark. Yukon and Shia joined him. I called Honey, who obediently returned to my side.

"Stay," I called to Denali. The last thing I wanted to happen was for him to engage in a scuffle with a grizzly. I could tell we'd surprised the grizzly as much as he surprised us. He reared up on his hind legs, reminding us of who was boss. I called the dogs at the front of the pack back to me, and fortunately, they obeyed. The bear obviously didn't want to deal with a pack of dogs who were all barking at him, so after sending a warning growl in our direction, he returned to four legs and trotted off into the trees. I kept my finger on the trigger of my rifle, hoping very much that I wouldn't have to use it. I'd fired off many warning shots in my day, but so far, I'd never had to kill an animal in order to protect myself.

After I returned to my cabin, I gave all the dogs and cats food and freshened their water. I checked on the animals in the barn to confirm their habitats were clean, they had enough food to tide them over until this evening, and their water bowls were full of fresh water. Having both a cougar and a grizzly in the immediate area meant Serena would need to be extra careful. I was confident she could handle herself, but I was tempted to call Jake and ask him to walk the dogs and tend to the animals in the barn. Serena would be fine inside the cabin, but I didn't want her to have the need to leave my property.

When I called Jake's cell phone, he didn't answer, so I tried Neverland. Wyatt answered and shared that Jake had gone somewhere with Sarge and wasn't expected to return until the bar opened at four. I shared my concerns and request with Wyatt so he could explain things to Jake in case I couldn't get ahold of him before leaving town. When I was done explaining everything, Wyatt offered to stay at my house while I was away. I wasn't as worried about Wyatt meeting up with a cougar or grizzly as I was about Serena having the same encounter, so I accepted his offer. After a bit of back and forth with my friends, it was decided that Serena and Wyatt would share pet-sitting duties while I was away. Serena would take my bed, Wyatt would take the guest room, and when they walked the dogs and tended to the animals in the barn, they'd head out together as a team.

Not long after I'd arranged and confirmed everything, Houston arrived for our trip.

"You made it right on time," I said after he backed the truck up to my front door, and we began loading our supplies.

"It's been quiet in town now that the summer hiking and recreation season is behind us. We still have a few hunters in the area, but overall, things have fallen into somewhat of a lull. Did you remember dog food?" he asked.

"Actually, I didn't. Thanks for reminding me. I'm sure Yukon wouldn't have minded eating the canned stew I did remember to pack, but it's a good idea to have his regular dog food on hand."

"Bottled water?" he asked.

"I have two cases. I have plenty of fuel and nonperishable food products as well."

"Sounds like you're prepared for anything."

I nodded. "I've lived here long enough to know that being prepared for anything is the only way to ensure you stay alive."

"Are you all set with Serena?" he asked as we loaded the last of the supplies.

"I confirmed with her this morning. I noticed cougar tracks during my walk this morning, and the pack and I ran into a grizzly, so I decided to call Jake and ask him to fill in instead, but he was off somewhere with Sarge, so I talked to Wyatt, and he agreed to stay as well."

"And Serena was okay with that?"

"Sure. Why wouldn't she be? Wyatt and Serena have always gotten along."

Houston slammed his tailgate closed. "I guess I would be more comfortable with Wyatt being there for walks and trips to the barn. No offense to Serena. She's great with the animals, but she doesn't strike me as the sort to use a gun even if she needed to."

"I think that is an accurate impression. Serena is a sweetie, but I'm not sure she has what it takes to face down a grizzly. Not that facing down a grizzly is something anyone should do, but I think you know what I mean."

"I do."

Once the supplies were loaded in Houston's truck, I let all the dogs out one more time for a quick break, and then I gave everyone who wasn't going with us a treat before we headed out. It was an overcast day, but there hadn't been any precipitation to this point. In fact, we'd been having a dry autumn, and while there was snow high up on the mountain peaks, the terrain in the valley was dry.

"It's a gorgeous day," I said as we sped along the highway once we'd left Rescue behind. "I didn't realize there was so much fall color out this way."

"It does seem as if the trees have changed earlier this year than usual, but it is gorgeous."

I turned my head slightly to enjoy the view through my window. "I was chatting with Chloe the other day, and she told me that the trees along the river up near the mouth of the gorge are simply breathtaking. I was thinking about taking the dogs and doing some hiking up there, provided I have time to get up there before the leaves fall."

"If this trip goes as planned, I guess we could go hiking on Sunday," Houston suggested.

"I'd like that." I turned so I was facing him. "I appreciate you coming up here with me this weekend."

"I was happy to help. I've actually been thinking about planning a weekend away from the business of our lives for the two of us. I wasn't necessarily thinking camping, but this could work as well."

I smiled. "I'd love for us to have a weekend together. Things are slow at the bar this time of the year, so any time you can arrange to take off should work for me."

"I currently have help, and things are slow, so maybe next weekend. Although," Houston added, "I just remembered that I have a seminar in Fairbanks next weekend."

"I could come along," I suggested. "Maybe just hang out in the room and read while you're busy."

"I should have some free time if you don't mind me being tied up for most of the day on Saturday. If we drive over on Friday afternoon, we'll have Friday night, Saturday night, and all day Sunday."

"That sounds nice. I'd enjoy having a weekend away where I could sleep in, and my only responsibility would be to relax. Of course, I have the animals to consider. I hate to ask Serena to watch them two weekends in a row, but maybe Harley and Brando can stay at my place."

"If you can work it out, the offer to tag along with me is open," Houston confirmed.

An hour later, Houston veered from the main highway heading north to the less maintained road leading toward Grizzly Mountain. As long as you avoided the potholes, the road wasn't too bad when it was free of snow, but in the winter, when the pavement was covered with a sheet of ice, the road could be treacherous.

"It looks as if the clouds might be moving north," I said as I stared at the black sky in the distance. "I didn't think to check the weather report for the weekend."

"I checked it this morning, and it looks like we'll get some rain, but I think the snow level is pretty high. I doubt we'll hit any snow today, although I imagine it will likely snow at the mining camp."

"I guess we should keep an eye on the forecast," I said. "Even a four-wheel drive with tires with an aggressive tread can get into trouble if the snow decides to pile up."

The rain started when we were about halfway between Rescue and Grizzly Flats. It was a light rain, which didn't pose much of a threat at this point, so we continued forward. As long as nothing went wrong, I estimated that we should arrive in Grizzly Flats in time to check into the hotel and then have some dinner. A nice relaxing dinner, followed by what I hoped would be a restful sleep, should be exactly what I needed to prepare for the long day ahead of us tomorrow.

Chapter 8

Except for the fact I'd fallen asleep while Houston was on the phone, thereby ending our evening before it had even started, yesterday actually did play out pretty much as Houston and I hoped it would. We'd arrived in the town on schedule, checked into our room, walked down the street for dinner, and then returned to the room where I laid on the bed and promptly fell asleep while Houston made a few calls. I did manage to sleep through the night without interruptions from outsiders invading my dreams, which was nice, but by the time I finally clawed my way to a state of wakefulness, Houston had already taken the dogs out for their morning walk, so I'd missed the opportunity to enjoy his presence next to me.

Of course, while yesterday had gone as planned, today was shaping up to be a different sort of day altogether. We'd gotten an early start as we'd hoped to. The breakfast buffet, which was included in the price of the room, wasn't anything fancy, but the food was hearty and cooked well, and Houston and I both enjoyed it. Once we'd eaten, we took the dogs for another short walk before loading them in the backseat of Houston's extra cab truck. We slowly drove through town and began to speed up as we hit the outskirts. We were maybe two or three miles outside the town limits when we noticed the row of cars belonging to members of the Alaska State Police.

"Maybe we should pull over and see what's going on," I suggested as I noticed that in addition to the four cars marked as state police, there were at least two dozen civilian vehicles.

"Yeah, I had that same thought," Houston said, pulling over onto the shoulder. "Wait here with the dogs while I check it out."

I watched as Houston got out and walked over to where a man wearing a uniform was speaking to a small group of people. Houston must have introduced himself since he reached out a hand and shook the hand of the man wearing the uniform. The man Houston had greeted pointed into the distance and said a few words, which had Houston looking in that direction. I couldn't hear what Houston was saying, but I noticed that he pointed toward the truck. The officer said something, and Houston turned and walked back toward me. He slid into the truck after opening the driver's side door.

"It seems that two kids are missing. Ten-year-old boys who took off on dirt bikes after school yesterday and haven't been seen since. They brought the state police in, and a search party is out looking for them, but when I told the officer I spoke to that we had two dogs trained specifically for S&R work, he asked if we could help. I told him we'd be happy to."

"Of course. If those kids didn't find shelter last night, they'll likely be in bad shape. Do you want me to attempt to connect with them?"

"Actually, that would be great. I told Officer Nielson that we'd need a piece of clothing recently worn by each of the boys and a recent photo of each boy before we could get started. I guess the father of one of the boys had these items for his son and went to his truck to get them. The other boy's father, mother, and brothers are out with the search party, but Officer Nielson is trying to get ahold of them via radio. Let's get the dogs harnessed and ready to go while we wait for everyone to gather what we need."

I slid out of the truck, opened the back door, and called the dogs. I told them to sit and wait while I dug out the harnesses and started slipping them into place. Yukon and Kojak knew what was expected of them and began to quake in anticipation of the search as I got them ready. By the time I managed to get both dogs suited up, Houston returned with two pieces of clothing.

"I'm not sure which t-shirt goes with which child, but I don't suppose it matters."

"And the photos?" I asked.

He handed me two wallet-sized photos.

"Okay. I'm going to sit in the truck for a moment and try to focus. If I don't pick anything up right away, we'll feed the scents to the dogs and get started. I can always take a break and try again in a while."

"Sounds like a plan."

"What are the boys' names?" I asked.

"The blond is Joshua, and the boy with the black hair is Dawson."

"Okay," I said, taking a deep breath and blowing it out slowly. "Give me five minutes, and I'll see what I can pick up."

Sometimes, it took me a while to make a connection, but for some unknown reason, there were other times when I couldn't connect at all. If my target was both close by and receptive to what I was putting out there, then ideally, I should be able to pick up a vague echo at the very least that would allow me to know that the person I was hoping to connect with was alive and conscious.

"No luck," I said to Houston almost ten minutes later as I looked around the area, hoping to find a clue. "Let's see if the dogs can pick up a scent."

"There are a ton of mines and caves in the area," Houston said. "I know if I'd come across a mine or cave when I was ten, there's no way I'd have been able to avoid checking it out."

"If they accessed one of the mines in the area, they may be in real trouble. Let's get started. You said they had bikes?"

"Motorized dirt bikes."

"That'll make it harder for the dogs, but let's give them a chance. If the dogs come up empty, I can try to connect again, but I'm hoping the dogs will pick up a scent and take us to the correct location."

If the boys stayed on their motorbikes and hadn't gotten off for some reason, then picking up a scent would be more difficult, but if they had taken breaks and had gotten off to walk around, then maybe.

"Do we know with any degree of certainty that they came this way?" I asked Houston.

"The officer I spoke to didn't know with any certainty that they'd passed through here, but the little dirt road where all the cars are parked is used by off-roaders to access the area. Dawson's father had told the state police that Dawson had mentioned that he wanted to check out an old dumpsite off this road on several occasions."

"Okay, then let's get started and see where we end up."

Houston and I decided to feed the scent on the yellow t-shirt to Yukon and the scent on the green t-shirt to Kojak. Our chance of success was actually greater if each dog had only one scent to focus on. We figured the two boys were likely to be together, so feeding each dog one scent seemed to make sense.

The dogs both took off down the dirt trail once we told them to "find" Dawson and "find" Joshua. There were dozens of people out walking around looking for the boys, so I knew refreshing the scent often for each dog was imperative at this stage of the game. It took an hour, but eventually, Yukon alerted.

"He has something," I said to Houston. We gave the dogs another whiff of the t-shirts and told them to "find" the boy with the matching scent again. This time, both dogs seemed a lot more excited about the hunt.

As I suspected they would, the dogs led us to the opening of a deserted mine shaft. I called out, but neither boy answered. I supposed there were several reasons for this. The boys might be so deep into the mine by this point that they couldn't hear us or were injured and unable to answer.

"Let's check it out," I suggested. "We have flashlights and rope, so exploring the entrance should be safe. We can call the others to bring additional equipment if we find evidence that the boys entered this mine."

Houston was open to my plan. We cinched up both leashes so the dogs would have to walk right next to our leg, and then we slowly entered the mine.

"Hello," I called out. "My name is Harmony. Can anyone hear me?"

I waited for a minute, but there was no reply.

"The floor is pretty flat, and there's plenty of head clearance, so let's continue," I said.

"Watch for falling debris," Houston said as he and Kojak stepped further into the mine. After we had traveled approximately a hundred yards, there was a fork with tunnels venturing off in two different directions.

"Hello," I called out again.

This time, I heard a faint response from the tunnel to the right. I instructed Yukon to walk behind me and took several steps forward.

"My name is Harmony. Can you hear me?"

"Help. I need help. My friend is hurt."

I continued to walk forward very slowly until I noticed a spot where the floor gave way to a dark hole. "Are you down in the hole?" I called out.

"I am. We fell. Can you see me?"

I shone the flashlight down into the deep crevice. "Yes, I can see you."

"Can you get me out of here?"

I looked at Houston. He shook his head. "We don't have nearly enough rope with us. We need to call the others." Houston took out his radio, but there wasn't any reception in the mine. "I'll need to head back outside."

"Take the dogs with you. I'll stay right here and wait for the rescue team."

Houston hesitated.

"I'll be fine. I promise that I won't venture down there alone. I just want to continue talking with whichever boy I'm speaking to."

"Okay, but don't move until I get back."

Houston took both dogs and headed back toward the entrance. I knew that even once he radioed the state police, it would be a while before they made it to our location, so I called out to the boys once again.

I shone my flashlight down into the deep hole the boys had fallen into. "We're getting help. Just hang on."

"Please don't leave. I'm scared. It was really dark before you got here."

"I won't leave," I promised. "How did you end up down there anyway?"

"Joshua was walking in front and didn't notice that the floor had caved in until he fell. I tried to climb down to help him, but then I fell."

I was very tempted to try to climb down to the boys myself, but I had promised Houston I wouldn't move until he returned, and even if I hadn't promised, I didn't have the equipment necessary for a successful rescue.

"My friend went to get the rescue team. They're on the way," I called out. "I need you to just stay where you are. Someone will be here to help you soon."

"I'm scared," the boy said once again.

"I know. My name is Harmony. What's yours?"

"Dawson."

"Okay, Dawson, just hang on a little bit longer. You said that Joshua fell. Is he near you? Can you touch him?"

"No, he fell further than I did, so he's a level beneath me."

"How long has it been since Joshua spoke to you?"

"I don't know. A long time. Too long. Please hurry. It's really dark, and I'm really scared."

Houston came up from behind me. He was alone.

"Where are the dogs?" I asked.

"One of the men who was out looking for the boys came by, and when I told him what was going on, he offered to hang onto the dogs while I came back for you. The rescue crew is on the way. They have plenty of rope, and four men who actually worked these mines in the past are here and willing to go in for the boys. It's tight in here, and they'll need room to work, so we need to head back outside."

"Okay. I'm going to leave my flashlight." I looked down into the hole. "The rescue workers are on their way," I called down. "I'm going to go out to make room for them, so I'm going to go back out, but I am going to leave my flashlight shining down into the hole so you can see. Hang on just a little while longer."

"Please hurry."

"They're on their way, I promise."

Luckily, the rescue crew had plenty of rope and flashlights. A group of four men who had worked the mines in the past and had experience in that sort of environment volunteered to go in. We gave them a detailed description of where the boys were and how to reach them.

About fifteen minutes after the rescue crew headed inside, a woman frantically ran to me.

"Did the dogs find my boy?"

"They did. The floor gave way, and they fell," I answered. "Four men just went in for them. They had plenty of rope, and the boys aren't that far back in the mine, so someone should be coming out at any minute now."

The woman began to sob. I stood up and gave her a long, hard hug. I imagined that the past twelve hours, knowing that your child was out there somewhere in the darkness, had been pure hell. I wished I could say that I couldn't even imagine what she'd gone through, but the reality was that I knew exactly what she'd gone through. I'd experienced it for the first time on the night my sister, Val, had died during a rescue, and I'd experienced it many times since then when I'd been able to connect with the pain of family members anxiously waiting for news about their loved ones.

Chapter 9

While both boys had been found alive, things were still uncertain. Dawson was only slightly banged up, but Joshua had a severe head injury and was in critical condition. The rescue worker I spoke to assured me that Joshua was receiving the best medical care in the area and, hopefully, would be fine in the long run. Once the boys had been taken to the medical clinic, Houston and I returned to our own journey. Of course, with the long delay created by the rescue, we were now set to arrive at the ghost town we were headed toward late in the day rather than midday as we'd hoped.

"This road is worse than I remember," I said as we slowly made our way along the rutted dirt road.

"When was the last time you were here?" he asked.

"I guess it was eight or nine years ago. The team received a report that a hiker, who had been with a larger group who had camped at the ghost town on their way up the mountain, was missing. I guess this guy, who was all into the photography aspect of the trip, had wandered off while following a herd of caribou. Apparently, he became turned around and had been walking in circles, but he wasn't that far away, so the dogs found him within an hour."

"That's good to hear. I've never visited the ghost town before, but I've heard about it and am looking forward to checking it out. Based on the photos that I've seen, it appears that many buildings are still standing."

"Quite a few buildings survived the weather mostly intact, while others have been reduced to rubble. It's a somewhat eerie feeling to walk down the main street where so many buildings appear as they did seventy years ago."

"I understand that the mine closed in the nineteen forties."

I nodded. "Like many mining camps, the town sprung up overnight with the discovery of gold and then became deserted just as quickly when the mine closed down."

Houston stopped the truck when we came to a washed-out section of the road. "I don't think we can make it through here." He looked out his window to the west. "I guess we can try heading west and hopefully find a better place to cross."

"Once you get around this little section, it looks as if the road is okay ahead of us. I think heading west through the trees might be the best idea," I agreed.

"Hang on. It's going to get bumpy."

The entire ride had been bumpy once we'd merged onto the dirt road, but I knew what he meant. It was likely to get much worse before it got better.

It took a while, but Houston's plan worked in the end. Once we made it around the washed-out section and back onto the dirt trail we'd been following in the first place, we decided to stop and let the dogs run around a bit. They'd gotten a lot of exercise while we'd been helping locate and rescue the boys lost in the mine, but we knew that bouncing our way over the ruts in the road was tiring for all of us.

The higher we climbed up the mountain, the colder it got. I was already glad I'd brought so many clothes I could layer on.

"We probably won't have a lot of time to look around once we get there, and we're going to want to just spend the night rather than attempting this road after dark, so we might want to set up camp once we arrive this evening, and then take a look around in the morning."

"That sounds fine with me," I confirmed. "The camp was built on the side of a mountain, so there isn't a lot of flat ground other than the parcel where the small settlement had been built," I said. "We'll want to camp there."

By the time we reached the camp, the sun had begun its descent, and the temperature had started to drop. We let the dogs run around while Houston searched for wood to build a fire, and I began digging through our supplies to find the box with the food. Houston's truck had an extra-long cab, so we decided that there was room inside the camper shell for Houston, me, and the dogs to sleep. It would be cozy but a lot warmer than if we had the dogs sleep in the cab.

"You were right about the creepy feel of all those buildings just standing here empty," Houston said as he began to arrange the wood he found for a fire. "It almost feels like people would begin spilling out of the buildings and into the street if I stood here long enough."

"It is creepy, especially at night. When I was up here with the S&R team, we were here during the day, but when Val was alive, we came up here camping with some of her friends. When I slipped out of the tent late at night to take care of needs of a personal nature and noticed all those buildings silhouetted under a full moon, I began to imagine the ghosts of residents past living in those buildings and almost lost it completely."

"So, how old were you then?"

I shrugged. "I guess maybe around fifteen."

"I remember going on a camping trip with one of my best buddies when I was fifteen. It was supposed to be Randy and me, Randy's older brother, Rich, and one of Rich's friends, whose name escapes me. After

Rich and his friend ran into a group of cheerleaders who'd decided to go camping as a preseason bonding ritual, the two older boys took off and left Randy and me alone. At first, it was fine, but then we realized Rich had all the food."

"Oh no. What did you do?"

"Luckily, we had fishing poles and supplies, so we fished. We ate fish and nothing but fish for three days straight. I refused to eat fish for years after that."

"I can see how eating fish and only fish would get old, but at least you had the fishing poles."

"I guess it was good that Randy decided to bring them along at the last minute. We almost didn't, but while packing the car, Randy noticed his fishing stuff in his garage, grabbed the box everything had been stored in, and tossed it in the car's trunk."

Once Houston got the fire going, he set up the camp stove. I emptied canned stew into a pot and put it on the gas burner to warm up. While our evening meal wouldn't be elegant, it would be hot and hearty, and that was the best sort of meal to have on a cold Alaskan night.

"It's freezing out here," Houston said as he tossed a couple logs on the fire to build it up.

"It is colder than I anticipated, but we'll be warm inside the arctic sleeping bags I brought. Let's eat and then turn in. I'm hoping to get an early start in the morning, so it's probably a good idea to turn in early."

Houston stood with his back to the fire while he ate the stew and crackers I'd given him. "I guess the entrance to the mine must be up on the mountain," he commented.

"It is. You'll be able to see where the entrance has been boarded up once it gets light."

"Can you get up there? Is there a trail?"

"There is an old trail," I answered. "Like the road out here, no one has taken the time to maintain it, so it's a bit rough going, and if I remember correctly, it's steep as well. The first time I was here with Val and her friends, a few of us hiked up there, and I remember wondering how on earth the men who worked that mine made that trek every day. Talk about a difficult commute."

"I imagine you get used to it. I guess life was hard all around for the men and women who lived in this town during its short-lived life as a bustling mining town." He looked around the area. "It's not as if there is anything else out there. Or at least there wasn't until Grizzly Flats popped up at some point. Before that, the feeling of isolation must have been intense."

"I'm sure it was. If you head down what had been the main street at one point and walk to the end, there are all these foundations. The homes that were built on the foundations are gone. I'm not sure why the houses didn't survive when many buildings did, although I suppose the homes were quickly constructed and not necessarily built to last. Anyway, my point is the size of these homes. We're talking about entire homes no larger than my bedroom. And, of course, there was no running water. I tried to imagine living in one of those little homes when I was here before, but my mind simply wouldn't go there."

"I suppose, as we've just said, the men and woman who lived here were used to what they had and likely didn't find their way of life quite as hard as we imagine it was." Houston tossed each dog a couple crackers. "I guess we should feed them and then get cleaned up. It's warmer now that I've got the fire going, but I'd like to be ready to head inside before the fire dies down."

"Layers," I said. "The secret is layers."

Chapter 10

She stood next to a freshly dug grave as snow drifted gently toward the ground. She tied two sticks together with an old piece of leather to form a cross. She hadn't wanted it to end this way. She hadn't wanted to see the look of shock and betrayal in his eyes as he slowly inhaled his last breath. She hadn't wanted to kill him, and she hadn't wanted him to hate her as he slowly drifted away. She'd done her job and fulfilled her destiny, but she'd never be the same.

As I had every time I'd shared my dream state with this particular woman, I woke with a start.

"Are you okay?" Houston whispered in my ear as he wrapped my shivering body in his arms.

"I'm okay."

"Was it the dream again?"

I took a deep breath and nodded even though the space around us was pitch black. The dogs had woken and were beginning to move about. There wasn't a lot of room for anyone to move within the safety of the camper shell, so I gave the command for them to settle down and return to sleep.

"Do you want to talk about it?" Houston asked.

"No, not now. Maybe in the morning. The sun will be up in a few hours, and when it rises, we will too."

"Okay." He kissed my cheek, which was about the only patch of skin on my entire body that wasn't covered in layers of clothing. "If you aren't able to sleep and decide you do want to talk, just wake me. Otherwise, I'll see you in a few hours."

With that, the gentle snoring I'd been lulled to sleep by in the first place seemed to resume.

As I lay in the dark space, I listened to the sounds around me and considered the content of my dream. In the past, the dreams had always been about the woman waiting at the graveyard for someone to arrive. Tonight, the dream had skipped ahead to the final goodbye. If this woman had cared about this man, why had she killed him? The whole thing made no sense. I tried to remember what the woman I'd connected with in my dream state had been feeling. There was no question that she felt grief and deep sorrow for what had occurred, but there was also something else – relief and perhaps completion. I supposed that if she had been anticipating the final showdown, which she somehow believed must occur, then feeling relief that it was finally over would actually make sense.

I tried not to toss and turn as I lay quietly, waiting for the sun to appear. I'd hoped to be able to settle into a dreamless sleep, but I could see now that was unlikely to occur. The emotions stirred up during my dream were multifaceted and deeply felt. I supposed I should have known it would take a while for my mood to even out a bit.

"Are you awake over there?" Houston asked as the first breath of dawn began to lighten the night sky.

"I am. In fact, I never got back to sleep." I leaned up on an elbow. "It won't be long before we'll be able to walk around without the fear of stumbling in the dark."

Houston unzipped and removed his sleeping bag. "I'll let the dogs out and get the fire going. Take your time getting up. We'll look around at first light and then start back down the mountain before the storm brewing over the summit decides to blow in."

Houston was right to be worried about the storm. It had been hanging just beyond the summit of the mountain range ahead of us for most of the previous day, but based on the direction of the wind, I was sure that it was heading our way. I waited a few minutes after Houston left the truck for him to get the fire going, but since I didn't want to go back to sleep, after about twenty minutes, I took a deep breath and stepped out into the frigid morning.

"Coffee?" Houston handed me a mug of the strong coffee he'd made from water boiled on the camp stove and instant granules. It wasn't that I hadn't enjoyed camp coffee in the past, but I supposed I had gotten spoiled with the smooth taste of coffee brewed with the fancy machine Jake had given me for Christmas last year. "So what's the plan?" he asked after I'd taken a few sips of the hot liquid.

"In my dream last night, the woman I've been sharing thoughts or memories with was standing in front of a freshly dug grave. I feel as if this woman wants me to find this grave. In fact, until my dream last night, I didn't understand the compulsion to come up here and look around, but now that I'm here, I think I'm supposed to find what the woman left for me to find."

"The grave of the man she killed?"

I nodded.

"Why? Why does this woman want you to find this man's remains?"

"I'm not sure," I said, furrowing my brow. "It seemed as if the woman cared for this man. In fact, I'm pretty sure the emotion I felt as she waited for him was love, all tied up with regret. She cared about this man, and yet she killed him. Perhaps she simply didn't want his memory to be lost forever."

Houston frowned. "If she cared about him, why did she kill him?"

I wrinkled my brow. "It was her destiny. I don't understand the whole thing at this point, but I think that the woman wants me to find his remains."

"And then what?" he asked.

I bit down on my lip. "I'm not sure. I suppose that if the woman is communicating with me as I suspect, then she may want me to identify the man she buried in the unmarked grave and then provide this man with a proper burial."

I could tell by the expression on Houston's face that he had doubts about my interpretation of my dream, but he didn't argue. Instead, he just refilled our coffee mugs and began organizing the items we would need if digging up an unmarked grave really was on the agenda.

Once Houston had dug out a few supplies, we called the dogs and began our walk down the ghost town's main street toward the graveyard, which was located in the low-lying foothills at the base of the mountain on the other side of the town. As it had been in my dreams, the cemetery was in disrepair. Old headstones, crumbling with age, had been choked out by the weeds that grew up around stone borders. Most of the grave markers were simply made from wood or chiseled stone, and few remained intact enough to read the inscriptions.

"How do we know which gravesite to vandalize?" Houston asked. "Given the short time this area was actively populated, there are a lot more gravesites than I anticipated."

"The gravesite in my dream was near the cemetery but not part of the cemetery." I walked through the center of the fenced area, which had been littered with rocks and debris. "I think the woman in my dream buried her victim closer to the mountain. She tied two sticks together to make a cross. I doubt the cross survived, but we'd be remiss if we didn't look for it."

"Do you have a sense as to when this man was buried? Are we looking for a fresh grave or one that has been weathered by the elements for dozens of years?"

"I don't know when this all occurred, but I do know that in my dreams, the cemetery was already overgrown, so it would have been at some point after the town was deserted and the graveyard had fallen into disrepair." I paused and looked around, attempting to locate the exact spot where the woman in my dream last night had been standing. She was looking down at the gravesite, but I could see the foot of the mountain just beyond where she had been standing as she momentarily looked up. A light dusting of snow had settled into some of the little nooks and crannies on the mountain, causing an intricate pattern of dirt and snow. "I remember there being shrubs to the woman's left. The shrubs were dormant in my dream, but they didn't look to have been native. I suspect that someone planted them at some point. Perhaps someone who had lived here when the mine was open and the town was populated."

"There are shrubs that seem to serve as a border for the cemetery," Houston pointed out.

I walked toward the shrubs on the far north side of the graveyard. I then stood just north of the shrubs and looked toward the mountain. "I think this might be it."

Houston walked over to where I was standing. "Do you just want me to start digging?"

Did I? On the one hand, if I was wrong and a previous resident had been intentionally buried in the area, I hated to disturb their final resting place. On the other hand, I felt like the spot where the woman in my dreams had buried the man was outside the border of the main cemetery provided by the shrubs. Getting down on my knees, I placed my hands on the ground. I knew I wouldn't be able to connect with the victim since I could only connect with the living, but I hoped that by making this strong connection to the burial site, I could connect with the woman, who, to this point, had only appeared in my dreams. I noticed the little wooden cross while I was down on the ground. It was lying on its side and had been overtaken by the weeds, but I was relatively sure it was the same cross I had seen in my dream state.

"Yes, I think we should dig here. If we don't find anything, then I guess we will have wasted a little time. If we do find something, we'll need to figure out a way to have the remains identified."

I could tell that Houston wasn't thrilled with my plan, but in the end, he did dig.

The remains weren't buried all that deep. Maybe a couple of feet beneath the surface. The body was significantly decayed, making identification based on physical attributes impossible.

"I guess the fact that this man was buried directly in the ground rather than in a coffin of some sort does lend itself to the idea that we haven't dug up a resident of the little camp who was properly buried by his family. I'm not sure, however, how we're ever going to be able to prove that this man is the same man the woman in your dreams waited for and then eventually killed," Houston said.

I noticed a golden medallion lying amongst the skeletal remains. "I feel a bit like a grave robber by taking this, but I suspect this medallion might be the key to helping us solve this mystery." I stood up from my squatting position next to the body. "So what do we do now? Take him with us? Leave him as he is and send the state police up? Rebury him?"

Houston didn't answer right away. He looked up into the dark sky and frowned. "I think we need to pack up and head out. The storm seems to be coming in this direction. I suspect we have an hour at the most before the weather makes it impossible for us to leave." He looked at the shovel in his hand. "I say we rebury him to protect the remains from scavengers and the elements. If we can ID him, there might be family members who will want his remains. I suppose we can also call the state police, but if we do that, we're going to have to explain exactly how we knew there was a body buried here and why we dug it up after so many years."

"Yeah. Calling the state police probably isn't the best idea." I wrapped my arms around my body as the wind picked up. "Let's cover him up and then get out of here."

While Houston went to work covering the remains, I headed back to the truck to finish packing everything up. Houston had just returned from his chore when he paused to look down the mountain.

"It looks as if we're about to have visitors." Houston nodded toward a cloud of dust that had been kicked up by an approaching vehicle.

"I suppose there might be other sightseers interested in visiting a ghost town, but it seems early in the day for anyone to be all the way out here if they hadn't spent the night as we did." I watched the vehicle come closer. "It looks like Landon," I said once the truck got close enough that I could begin to make out the details of the make, color, and model that appeared to be flying down the rutted road Houston and I had taken our time driving on the previous day.

"I wonder what he wants," Houston commented.

"It can't be good," I said, urgent to know why he'd drive all the way out here but dreading the answer.

Houston and I waited as the truck approached. As soon as Landon arrived at our destination, I ran over to see what was going on.

"Dani and Jordan never came home from the village they visited on Friday," he explained. "We've been trying to reach them, but neither is answering our calls. Jake is worried and is hoping that you can connect with one or the other. We couldn't reach you on the phone, so he sent me to fetch you while he arranged for someone to fly us to the location where Dani and Jordan were last seen."

"No one has seen them since Friday?" I screeched.

Landon answered. "Jake told me that when Jordan left to meet Dani on Friday, the two of them were heading toward one of the native villages near Utqiagvik to deliver vaccines. Jordan told Jake that unless something unexpected was waiting for her, she'd be home by mid-afternoon that same day. When Jordan wasn't home by mid-afternoon, Jake didn't worry too much. There have been occasions when Jordan has been greeted by villagers who need additional treatment, but when that happens, she always finds a way to call and let him know there's been a change in her plans. When she still wasn't home by dark, he began to worry, but he knew Dani wouldn't risk flying if the weather was bad, so he figured he'd hear from her the following day. When they still weren't home by yesterday morning, Jake got more serious about tracking them down. He was able to contact the man Jordan works with to organize visits to this particular village. The man told Jake that when Jordan heard about a boy who'd had a bad fall and had suffered a head injury in a nearby village, she informed him that she was going to stop there and take a look at the child before heading home. He said

Dani and Jordan left his village around two o'clock on Friday. He also said that a storm was blowing in, so it was possible they were waiting it out."

"I suppose that if the boy was in bad shape, she might have stayed, but it does seem as if she would have found a way to let everyone know what was going on," I said. "Jordan has a satellite phone, and while she does have problems with service when the weather is bad, she can usually find a way to get through."

"I take it that Jake tried contacting Dani on her radio?" Houston asked.

"Jake has tried everything."

"Okay," I said. "I'm not sure if this will work, but I'm willing to try. I'm going to need a quiet place to work, so I'm going to lay down in the back of the truck."

Once I was settled, I closed my eyes and focused on Dani. I could have chosen either friend, but Jordan was much more analytical than Dani, and I figured she was the least likely of the pair to allow me in. I pictured Dani's sweet face in my mind as I desperately tried to make a connection. After at least twenty minutes of trying and getting nothing, I decided to switch and focus on Jordan. I was already tired, and my head was pounding. I figured I might have ten more minutes before I'd need to take a break.

Jordan, it's Harmony. Can you hear me?

I took a few deep breaths as I focused intently on her face.

If you can hear me, just relax and let me in.

I tried to reach Jordan for another twenty minutes but then admitted defeat. The reality was that it had been months since I'd been able to connect with anyone. At least intentionally. I seemed to have been connected with the woman in my dreams, but other than my connection with this particular woman during my dream state, I'd had zero luck connecting with anyone else.

"I'm sorry, but I wasn't able to connect with either Dani or Jordan," I said to the men.

Landon responded. "Jake will be waiting for our call. Let's head back to Grizzly Flats, where we will have access to a landline and call Jake. If there's a flight north to be had, he should have had time to secure it by now."

Chapter 11

By the time we made it to Grizzly Flats and were able to call Neverland, Sarge informed us that Jake had already chartered a plane, and he and Wyatt were on their way to Utqiagvik. I, of course, wanted to find a way to head north as well, but the storm had worsened in the past hour, and it looked as if no one would be leaving Grizzly Flats via any mode of transportation in the near future.

"I'm not good at waiting," I said to Houston and Landon after we'd checked into the hotel and then walked down the street to grab something to eat.

"I don't disagree with you, but I'm not sure there's anything we can do until the storm lets up a bit," Landon said. "According to Sarge, the storm is a lot worse to the north of us than it is here, and it's pretty bad here. The only way to access the village where Dani and Jordan were last seen is via air, and there's no way any pilot will attempt flying until the weather clears a bit."

"Do you think they just got caught up in the storm?" Houston asked. "The intel we've been provided suggests that Jordan heard about a child who needed her services in a small village outside Utqiagvik. If she was there when the storm hit, she might have decided to wait it out and stay where she was until the storm blew through."

Even though I knew Houston was most likely right, that didn't make waiting any easier.

"After we eat, I'm going to attempt to connect again," I informed the men.

Houston looked at me. "How's your head?"

"It still hurts, but the aspirin is kicking in, and the food will help."

Once we reached the little eatery, I ordered a turkey club with extra bacon and avocado. "This is good. I have to admit that I didn't expect a small café all the way up here to have real avocados. I was expecting some sort of a spread, but this is the real deal, and it's fresh."

"It does look good," Houston agreed as he took a bite of his roast beef and provolone sandwich.

"I wonder if Jake and Wyatt made it to Utqiagvik okay," Landon said. "The storm is bad."

"If Jordan left Utqiagvik to treat a child in a neighboring village, then there must be someone in

Utqiagvik who knows specifically where our friends went," I said.

"I'm surprised Jake hasn't called us by now. It's been hours," Landon added.

I glanced out the window at the whiteout conditions. "If it's still snowing this hard up north, I suppose Jake will need to wait a while to head out, but I'm sure he'll call before he heads away from Utqiagvik. If he hasn't called by the time we finish our meal, we'll try to call him."

Once we finished lunch, we bundled up and returned to the hotel. We'd left the dogs in the room that Houston and I were sharing, so we suggested to Landon that he join us there while we waited. Once we'd let the dogs out for a fast bathroom break, we gathered around the little table in the corner of the room and tried to decide what to do. The reality was that while we were all the sort to want to take action, there wasn't anything any of us could do. At least, not until the storm let up.

"I'm going to call Jake," I said. "I know he said he'd call us once he figured out what was going on, but it's been a long time, and I'm done waiting."

Unfortunately, Jake didn't answer when I called his cell phone, so I left a message. I then called Wyatt, who I figured was with Jake, and could get a message to him, but he didn't answer either. Sometimes, the cell network was wiped out completely when we had severe storms. I had a feeling that might be the case.

"You look tired," I said to Landon.

"I was up all night. I suppose I could use some rest."

"You should go to your room and have a nap. If we hear anything, we'll come and bang on your door," Houston suggested.

Landon yawned. "That sounds like a good idea. I suppose that whatever comes next is going to be tiring. Even if the only task assigned to me is to head back to Rescue once the storm clears, the drive back is going to be three times as bad as the drive here was."

It was true that once the snow fell, traveling in regular motor vehicles was almost impossible in this part of the state.

After Landon left, I decided to attempt to connect with either Jordan or Dani again. I knew I'd had zero luck connecting to victims in the past couple of months, but Dani and Jordan were friends, and I figured they'd be listening for me if they were in trouble. I knew I couldn't do anything to help either friend at this point, but if I was able to connect, I figured that I could at least get an update on their current status.

Once Houston helped me get comfortable on the bed, he laid down next to me and held my hand. Before my recent dry spell, I had been getting better at connecting without an anchor, but today had been a particularly trying day, and I felt like I might be at the end of my rope.

"Ready?" he asked me.

I nodded and then closed my eyes. *Dani? Jordan? Can either of you hear me?*

I waited, but there was no answer.

I continued to try. I wasn't sure exactly what was going on, but I was beginning to think that my gift had simply gone away as abruptly as it had appeared.

Dani, Jordan? I held their names and images in my mind but was getting nothing.

"The phone," Houston said, breaking my concentration. He got up and answered. "It's Jake."

I waited while Houston spoke to him.

"What's he saying?" I asked.

Houston held up a hand, indicating that I should wait with my questions for him to finish his phone conversation. After he hung up, he looked at me.

"Jake and Wyatt made it to Utqiagvik. They've been able to confirm that after Jordan had met with those she planned to meet with in Utqiagvik, she and Dani had left via snowmobile for a neighboring village. Jake and Wyatt rented snowmobiles and safety gear and went to the village that Jordan had been heading toward, but when they arrived, they found out that while Dani and Jordan had been there, the pair had left to head back to Utqiagvik after treating the child who they'd made the trip to help. At this point, no one knows what happened to them after they left the village. The chopper is still where Dani left it when they arrived Friday morning, so we know they never made it back to the chopper after leaving the village."

"If the storm was bad, they may have found a place to wait it out," I said.

"That would have been the best move, but if they made it back to Utqiagvik, they should have been able to call and let someone know what they were doing."

"I just have this feeling they are in trouble," I said. "I have nothing to base my feelings on and no way of knowing that with any certainty, but I feel it in my gut."

"Are you surprised that you haven't been able to connect with either friend?" Houston asked.

"No," I admitted. "Not really. It's been months since I've been able to connect with anyone other than the woman in my dreams. I feel like her presence might be blocking things."

"We found the body of the man she killed," Houston said. "What more does she want from you?"

"I'm not sure," I admitted. "Maybe she wants me to find a way to understand what happened."

"Considering the fact that the man had been in the ground for a very long time, that seems like a big ask."

I didn't disagree with that. "I'm going to try to connect again," I said. "I realize I already tried and failed, but this is too important. Our friends' lives might depend on my finding out where they are."

I tried several times over the next few hours. I'd focus my attention for as long as I could before the pain in my head became too much to bear, and then

I'd take a break and try again. Apparently, I'd fallen asleep the last time I laid down and tried to connect because the next thing I remember was waking up with a gasp.

"What is it?" Houston asked, hurrying over to the bed from the table where he'd been sitting.

"I fell asleep. I had a dream," I said, pushing up onto my elbows.

"A vision?" he asked.

I frowned. "I'm not sure. I think so, but it doesn't fit. In my dream, there was a woman sitting in a rocking chair next to a fireplace, speaking to a young girl. I was experiencing the dream through the eyes of the girl, so I can't say how old she was with any degree of certainty, but I suspect she was old enough to understand what the woman was saying but not old enough to fully comprehend what might happen next. I feel like the dream might be related to the other dreams I've been having about the woman in the cemetery, but I can't be sure."

"You said the woman in the rocking chair was talking to the child. Do you know what was being said?"

I closed my eyes and tried to remember. "No. I don't remember what the woman said, but I do remember that the woman was filled with anger, and the child was filled with deep sorrow." I sat up the rest of the way and spun around so my feet were on the floor. "Any luck getting through to Jake?"

"I tried calling him, but he didn't pick up, so I sent him a detailed text. Sometimes, texts are able to go through when calls can't. He texted back and said that one of the villagers told him that Dani and Jordan were confronted by a man who lives in a cabin about a two-hour snowmobile ride from his closest neighbor as they were leaving the village. The villager Jake spoke to overheard the man telling the women who came to help the boy that he needed help for his mother. He was pretty sure that Dani and Jordan went with this man."

"So if Jake knows where they are, he can go to them."

"Jake says he plans to check it out, and he hopes they are where the villager thought they might be, but he can't do anything until the storm passes. As has already been mentioned, the storm is a lot worse up north than it is here."

"Did Jake say if he knew how to get to the cabin?"

"He didn't say, but I'm sure he'll do whatever needs to be done to find out."

Since Houston got through to Jake via text, I figured I could as well. I texted Jake and asked him to call or at least text me back. The waiting was making me nuts, but the reality was that there was nothing I could do to help at this point.

"So what now?" I asked Houston.

He shrugged. "I guess all we can do is wait to hear from Jake. I was going to research the medallion we found in the grave, but I haven't been able to secure an internet connection. I noticed a deck of cards sitting on the bedside table."

"Cards? You want to play cards?"

"Not really, but I want to take your mind off the waiting."

I supposed it was nice of Houston to try, but the last thing I wanted to do was get involved in a silly card game. I was about to suggest that we try some TV when my cell phone dinged. "It's Jake texting me back. They know where the man who the villager saw speaking to Jordan lives. Since there aren't any roads to the cabin, the only access is by snowmobile, cross-country skis, snowshoes, or helicopter. Dani's chopper is still where she left it, so using it to access the cabin where the man and his mother live makes the most sense, but they need to find a pilot and then wait for the storm to die down a bit. He promised to text or call when he knows more."

"It sounds as if Jake is on top of things. Based on what we know, it sounds as if Dani and Jordan simply went with this man to help his mother, and then the storm hit, so they decided to wait it out."

"I hope that's all it is." I got up and began pacing around the room. Both dogs watched me intensely, trying to figure out if we were going for a walk or what was happening.

"The woman who runs the hotel told me that she'd bring dinner up to our room," Houston shared after neither of us had spoken for a while.

"Dinner? Didn't we just have lunch?"

"It's been hours. I texted Landon, and he's going to join us once the food arrives. I think he's going even more stir-crazy than we are."

I looked at the dogs. "I should take them out for a quick break."

"I can take them," Houston offered.

"I could use the fresh air."

"How about we go together."

The wind had picked up, and the snow was coming down heavily. Seeing more than a few feet in front of you was impossible, so we encouraged the dogs to be quick about things. Once we returned to the room, Houston sat at the desk and tried to find an internet connection that might be working despite the storm.

"Still no luck?"

"Not really. I had an internet connection for about fifteen minutes, but it's gone again." He held up the medallion we'd found at the cemetery. "It appears that the image on the front is an insignia. The design is fairly intricate, but the presence of the hammer and pick seems to make it appear that the man was connected to the mine, which makes sense." He turned the medallion over. "There's a word on the back. The word is fiútestvér. I looked fiútestvér up during the fifteen minutes the internet worked and learned that it's Hungarian for brother. So far, I haven't found a reference to this particular symbol online, but I'm hoping that if we can identify the medallion as having been the official crest of a group, we'll be able to identify the man buried in the shallow grave near the cemetery."

I sat on one of the chairs surrounding the small table where Houston was working. "By the time this storm is over, I imagine the graveyard will be covered with several feet of snow. Going back for the body, if that's even what we decide to do, probably won't be possible until the snow melts, which at that elevation is likely to be June at the earliest." I picked the medallion up. "While I am hoping that identifying the man buried there will be enough to stop the dreams, at this moment, I'm more worried about Dani and Jordan."

"Yeah, me too. I guess focusing on the medallion just gave me something to do since we seem to be in a waiting pattern."

"Do you think they're okay?"

"I think they are." Houston put his hand over mine. "It sounds as if our dinner is here," he commented after we heard a clanging sound in the hallway. "I'll text Landon and tell him to come on over."

As we ate, we discussed the situation and how we could help. There wasn't anything that could be done until the storm let up. Once that happened and Jake was able to head to the cabin where the villager had told him his friends might be, I hoped that he would find them alive and well, but I had no idea how I would keep my cool until then.

Chapter 12

It took a while, but I was finally able to fall asleep, and at some point during the night, I was able to make the connection I'd been trying to make all day. I wasn't sure why I could only connect in my dream state, but that seemed to be a new development I would need to try to process.

"Harmony? Is that you?" I could hear Jordan say aloud.

It is. You don't have to speak. Just think about what you want to say.

"Dani and I are in trouble."

Are you hurt?

"I'm fine. Dani is unconscious but stable for the moment."

I wanted to ask what happened. I wanted to ask how Dani's injury occurred, but I knew the most important thing was to find them, so instead, I asked where they were.

"I'm in a room with an old woman who is dying," Jordan continued. "I'm not sure where we are exactly. Dani and I had just left the village where I'd headed to help a child who needed my services when a man approached and told me that his mother was gravely ill. He insisted that I go with him, so I agreed to do so. Dani came with me."

Is the cabin close to the village?

"No. I thought it would be, but it's not. The man who came for me had a snowmobile, as did we. Once we entered the forest, I got turned around, but I would estimate it took us two hours to get here. When we finally arrived at the isolated cabin, I found a very old woman unconscious in a bed. I told the man that the woman was likely dying and that the only chance she had was to get her to a hospital. He told me he wouldn't allow her or us to leave and that I needed to help her. When Dani tried to force her way out of the cabin, he hit her on the side of the head with his rifle. It all happened so fast. The man is strong. Dani passed out and has been drifting in and out of consciousness ever since. Even if I could find an opportunity to slip away, I would never leave Dani here. I'm scared, and I don't know what to do."

Do you think Dani has a brain bleed?

"I can't be sure at this point, but the fact that she regained consciousness, even if it was just for a short time, is encouraging."

And the woman you are there to help?

"Dying. The woman is in a coma. I found out that she's ninety-two years old. In my opinion, her body is simply shutting down. I've tried to tell this man that there isn't anything I can do to save her, but each time I tell him that or mention that Dani and I really need to leave, he makes a comment about making sure the woman lives if my friend and I want to live. The guy simply refuses to listen to anything I have to say. If Jake doesn't find us soon, I'm not sure what is going to happen."

So, is the woman in the bed this man's grandmother?

"Mother. I'd say the man holding us is somewhere between sixty and sixty-five. He's a large man. Strong. He seems to be uneducated. At one point, he said something about having lived in the cabin with his mother his entire life."

Okay, just hang on. One of the villagers saw you with the man and told Jake where to find you. The storm is bad, so he needs to wait for it to pass. As soon as it does, he'll come for you.

"Okay. Hurry. I'm not sure if we'll be able to connect again. I've been reaching out to you but haven't had any luck until now."

Are you sleeping?

"No. I came in to check on the woman. She was restless, so I held her hand, and when I did, I sensed you."

With that, she was gone, and I opened my eyes and sat up.

"Are you okay?" Houston asked. I must have awakened him with my tossing and turning.

"I connected with Jordan during my sleep. Or I guess she connected with me." I paused to think about that for a moment. Jordan had said she was in the old woman's bedroom, holding her hand, when she felt my presence. Maybe the woman with Jordan was the same woman I'd been psychically connected with. If that was true, then perhaps she'd acted as a conduit. "Anyway," I continued, realizing that I was never going to figure all of that out at this point, and perhaps it didn't really matter. "Jordan doesn't know where they are, only that they traveled for about two hours to arrive at their destination, but it sounds like they are in the cabin the villager told Jake about. She said that Dani was hurt. She was hit in the head with a rifle."

"That doesn't sound good."

"It's not, but she did say that Dani regained consciousness for a while, and while she certainly isn't out of danger, it was a good sign that she was conscious and able to talk until she slipped away again."

"Jordan must be terrified."

I nodded. My head felt like it would literally explode, so I laid down until the pounding stopped.

"Can I get you anything?' Houston asked, worry evident in his tone.

"No. I just need to lay here for a few minutes."

"I'm going to try Jake again," Houston said. "I know you tried and couldn't get through, but the poor guy must be frantic by this point. I know I'd be frantic if you were the one who was missing. I figure the fact that you were able to connect with Jordan will give him a degree of comfort."

I just lay there in the dark with my eyes closed. I wasn't sure what time it was, but it had to be in the middle of the night. I wasn't surprised that Houston wanted to text Jake with the news, but I was surprised when Jake answered immediately. The poor guy likely hadn't been able to sleep.

"What did he say?" I asked.

"He said he was happy that you connected with Jordan and that they seemed to be on the right track. He said that while it's still dark, the storm is letting up, and he and Wyatt plan to head out at first light."

"Did they find a pilot?"

"I don't know. Jake didn't say, and I didn't ask, but he would like you to try connecting with Jordan again once you feel you're up to it. He's worried that the woman will die and that the man will take his anger out on Dani and Jordan before he and Wyatt can get there."

"Did he say anything more about the man and the dying woman?" I wondered.

"No, we only communicated by text, so even if Jake knows more about the situation, I doubt he'd wanted to go into a long explanation via text message." He put a hand on my cheek. "How's your head?"

"Better. I'm going to get up and walk around for a minute, and then I'll try contacting Jordan again, even though I've had no luck connecting with anyone intentionally. The only connections I've made in months have been while I was asleep, and the dreams came to me rather than me initiating the connection."

"You sound worried that you haven't been able to initiate connections."

"I guess I am to a point. My gift isn't something I asked for, and it isn't something I necessarily wanted, but it has served me well. I feel as if I've been able to save lives that might not have been saved had I not been able to make connections. I don't understand why I no longer have the ability to initiate a connection, but I hope this is just a temporary glitch."

Houston put an arm around me and hugged me before he turned the bedside lamp on and sat up. He picked his cell phone up off the bedside table and looked at it.

"According to my weather app, the storm north of us is beginning to clear," Houston informed me. "It looks like we have another seven or eight hours of heavy snow, but if the app is correct, Jake might be able to head out the next hour or so."

"I'm going to text him again," I said. "It's almost four a.m., which is later than I thought. I'm going to text Landon and see if he's awake. If he's not, he'll get the text when he wakes up. Either way, I'll ask him to join us. I have a feeling the next few hours are going to be intense."

Landon was awake when I texted and agreed that it would be nice to have company while we waited to hear whether Jake was able to make it to the cabin where we believed Dani and Jordan were being held. He wanted to wash up a bit but assured me he'd come by our room. Once I had made arrangements with Landon, I tried to call Jake again. The call went directly to voicemail. I decided to try another text, but Jake called me before I was halfway through typing it out.

"Jake. I'm so happy to hear from you. Are you heading out?"

"The service is going in and out, so I need to talk fast. As I shared in my text, once I explained that Dani and Jordan had been taken by a man who lived alone with a very old woman in an isolated cabin that was about a two-hour snowmobile ride from here, several locals knew who I was talking about. It took some doing, but we found someone to fly Dani's chopper. There's been a break in the storm, so we're heading out as soon as the pilot arrives. I'm hoping that we will be able to land close to the cabin. If all goes as planned, we should be there within the hour. I need you to attempt to connect with Jordan and let her know that we're on our way. There's no telling what the man who kidnapped Dani and Jordan will do when they hear the chopper, so it will be best if Jordan is prepared."

"Okay. I'll try again as soon as we hang up." I decided not to point out that I'd had zero luck initiating a connection since I didn't want to worry him more than he already was. "Be careful and call me once you have them."

With that, he hung up, and I did as well.

I shared the content of my call with Jake with Houston and laid down on the bed again. I closed my eyes and concentrated. I was looking for Jordan, but what I got was a connection to the old woman in the coma. I hadn't been sure before, but this time, I was sure that the woman in the coma was the same woman I'd been connecting with for the past few weeks.

It is you, I said to the woman. *You are the one who killed the man in the cemetery.*

"It was my destiny. I wish I had time to explain, but I fear I have only moments left in this life. Tell my son that I love him. Tell him I'm sorry for locking him away in this cabin with me. I didn't mean to do him harm, but I found I was unable to deal with the world after having done what I had. My son was innocent in all of this. I should have tried harder to give him a normal life. I'm afraid that it is much too late for that. I can't change decisions that have already been made, but I do want him to be safe and happy. Tell him I love him. Tell him it is my time to go, and I am at peace with that."

I was about to respond, but I could sense her life force slipping away as she focused her mind on happier times. Time spent with her son when he was a child. Time spent with her own mother when she was a child. The images flowed gently like a leaf on a river until her mind settled on a single image of a dark-haired woman standing at a gravesite with a child. I instinctually knew that the child in my memory was the woman I was connected with.

"Never forget the pain that has been ours to bear," the dark-haired woman said to the child. "Never forget the man who took your father from those of us who needed him most. Never forget that vengeance for his loss is the only way." She squeezed the child's hand until the child felt sure that her delicate bones would break. "It is your destiny and your responsibility to make things right. To avenge the man who was lost. Do you understand?"

"Yes, Grandmother," the child answered.

"A son for a son," the woman insisted. "It can end no other way."

With that, the woman was gone.

I opened my eyes.

"What is it?" Houston said.

"The woman I've been meeting up with in my dreams. The woman who killed the man and buried his body near the cemetery. She is definitely the same woman who the man who took Dani and Jordan hoped to save."

"The old woman in the coma?" Houston asked.

I nodded. "She's gone now. She died while we were connected."

"You intentionally connected with her?" Houston asked.

"No, I was trying for Jordan but got her instead. She connected with me. She somehow knew she had only moments left. She needed me to see her life. She needed me to understand. She is afraid for her son. He has never been without her. She wanted me to make sure he was taken care of."

"He'll likely go to jail once Jake catches up with him."

"I know what he did was wrong. I know he kidnapped two of our friends and hurt Dani. But it appears he was born to the old woman in that cabin well away from anyone else and has lived in that cabin with his mother for his entire life. He is frightened. Faced with uncertainty, he chose the single course of action that came to mind. He tried to save her, but in the end, nothing he could do would stop the passage of time and the inevitable end we all must face."

Landon knocked on the door, and Houston called for him to come in. I took a few minutes to catch him up. Connecting with the old woman in her final moments had about done me in. Her destiny had been thrust upon her at an early age. A destiny she didn't ask for and certainly didn't want, but one that she had been taught from an early age was hers to fulfill in order to enact justice for the death of her father. I still wasn't clear about what that all meant. She hadn't had time to explain, although I could sense she wanted to.

"We need to attempt to get ahold of Jake again," I said.

"I've been trying, but he's out of range," Houston informed me.

"Jordan. She needs to know that the woman is dead and that Jake is on his way. There is no telling what the son will do once he realizes what is happening."

My head was already pounding, and my energy was stripped, but I knew I had to attempt to reach Jordan again. I lay on the bed again, closed my eyes, and tried to focus. If the old woman had died in the past few minutes, I knew that Jordan likely had her hands full. It would be hard to get her attention, but I needed to try. I figured that if my connection with the old woman had been blocking my ability to connect with anyone else, then now that she had passed, I should be free of her grip. Apparently, I was wrong.

Chapter 13

It had been four days since Jake had rescued Dani and Jordan. Dani had been taken to the hospital but had since been released and was doing fine. Jordan had taken a few days off after her ordeal but was back to work by this point. The man who had kidnapped my friends had been arrested, but the man who was in charge of law enforcement for the area knew the story of the man who was born and then raised in the little out-of-the-way cabin and vowed to try to find an alternative to prison. I still wasn't sure if I'd discovered whatever the woman in my head wanted me to find, but at this point, I simply hoped that my nightmares had come to an end and my ability to initiate a connection would return to normal. So far, the dreams had stopped, but my gift had not returned despite the fact the team had been called out on two rescues this week, neither of which I'd been able to help with in my usual manner.

"What's going on with the lights?" I asked Wyatt after I arrived at Neverland for my dinner shift.

"The breaker keeps tripping. Jake called the electrician, who is taking care of another call but has assured him that he will be out as soon as he can get here."

"Has Jake tried flipping it back himself?"

"About a hundred times. It just blows again. Jake doesn't want us seating anyone until we find out what's going on. Luckily, no customers have tried to come in, so it hasn't been a problem. It should be slow today, but if the electrician can't fix it by five, we'll need to put a sign on the door letting our customers know we'll be closed for the day."

I slipped onto a barstool. "I hope the electrician gets here soon."

"Yeah, me too. It will be boring to just stand around all night waiting to see what's going to happen." Wyatt held up the cola he'd been sipping on. "Do you want something to drink?"

"Just some sparkling water, please."

He turned and put ice in a glass and then used his wand to fill it with sparkling water.

"As long as you're here and not busy, I wanted to ask you about this weekend. Houston and I had made plans to head to Fairbanks this weekend before the whole thing with Dani and Jordan happened. He's supposed to attend a seminar, and he figured we could combine the seminar with some couple time. I wasn't sure we were still going to go after everything that happened, but I spoke to him this morning, and he said he's still planning to go and hoped I'd still want to come along. On the one hand, getting the time off is no problem since it's been so slow, although I feel bad about leaving the animals alone for two weekends in a row. On the other hand, finally having some one-on-one time with Houston sounds like much too perfect of an opportunity to pass up, so I'm thinking about tagging along as I originally planned. If I do go, are you game to hang out at my cabin and help Serena with the animals again this weekend?"

"I am as long as you're back by Tuesday. I'm heading to Bryton Lake to meet with Timber's trainer Tuesday morning."

I smiled. "I wasn't aware that this whole thing was happening so fast, but I'm excited to meet our new team member, and I'm really excited that you will be the one to work with him. And Houston and I will be back on Sunday, so that shouldn't be a problem."

"Are you heading out tomorrow?"

I nodded. "In the afternoon. We're just staying for two nights, and Houston has the seminar on Saturday, so it's going to be a quick trip, but the more I think about it, the more I realize that I really am looking forward to it."

"It's a nice change of pace to mix things up every now and then."

"It is. So everything went smoothly last weekend with you and Serena acting as co-pet sitters?"

He smiled. A lazy yet content sort of smile. "Everything went great. In fact, Serena and I had a lot of fun. I've known her for a while, but until this past weekend, I didn't realize what a good sense of humor she has."

I didn't think of Serena as having an exceptional sense of humor, but she was alone with Wyatt for two nights, so perhaps they'd had the chance to talk and get to know each other.

"Are you taking any of the dogs with you this time?" he asked.

"No. As I indicated, Houston will be busy on Saturday, so I'll need to entertain myself. I might even do some shopping and sightseeing. I don't want to worry about the dogs if I go sightseeing. Which reminds me, Houston plans to leave Kojak at the cabin. I hope that's okay."

"That's fine. Kojak is a cool dog, and he minds well. It seems like you've been tired lately. I think a few days away will do you good."

"I think so as well."

"Are you still blocked telepathically?"

I nodded. "I'm not sure what's going on. The last time I was able to connect with anyone at will was a few months ago when we all went out looking for the group of teenagers who'd been kidnapped. My gift seemed to be working fine at that point, but, with the exception of the connection I had with the old woman who had been haunting my dreams for weeks before she passed, I haven't been able to connect at all since then."

"And you haven't had any dreams or visions since she died?"

I shook my head. "Not a one. And I've really tried."

And boy, had I tried. And tried and tried and tried.

"You connected with Jordan when she was trapped in the cabin with the old woman and her son," Wyatt pointed out.

"I did, and at the time, I thought the reason I had connected with her was because I was asleep, but Jordan told me that she'd been holding the old woman's hand when she became aware of me, so now I'm thinking it was this woman who provided the conduit that was needed to connect with Jordan in the first place."

"And now that she's dead, shouldn't you be free of her?"

I shrugged. "I would think so, but I still don't have my powers. To be honest, I have absolutely no idea what might happen next."

"So, no rumblings at all?"

I shook my head. "So far, it's been nice and quiet in my head. In a way, I guess I almost appreciate that. You know how much making a connection always takes out of me. But then I think about all the people I've been able to save or offer comfort to since my gift first appeared, and I realize that I really would like to figure out how to get it back."

Wyatt refilled my sparkling water. "You said that the old woman has been the only individual that you have been able to connect with since the missing teens. Were you able to connect intentionally or only in your dreams?"

"Only in my dreams. I haven't had a single vision outside my dream state since we went looking for the missing teens this past summer."

Wyatt began wiping the already clean bar top. "Maybe you aren't free from whatever sort of hold this woman had on you because you haven't yet completed whatever she wanted you to do."

I took a sip of my sparkling water and then replied. "I've thought about that, but at this point, I'm not sure what more I can do."

Wyatt crossed his arms and leaned on the counter. "Maybe you can start by trying to expand your knowledge base. During our talk with the villager who pointed us to the cabin the woman and her son lived in, he shared that the woman's name was Destiny. Destiny Kellerman. Her son was called Bucky, although the villager wasn't sure if that was his real name. He didn't know much about the woman, only that she had lived there with her son for decades. In fact, he seemed to think that Bucky might have been born in that cabin."

"The woman said as much at one point. I can't imagine how it must have been for the boy to be brought up in such isolation. I mean, he had no one other than his mother for company from the moment he was born until the moment she died. No wonder he was so desperate to save her. The poor guy must be totally lost."

"Yeah," Wyatt breathed. "I really did feel bad for the guy. The man from the village said that Bucky would come into town for supplies from time to time, and there were a few merchants who would stop and chat with him, so if he's given a chance and isn't sent to prison, he does have a small base from which to begin to build normal relationships."

"Houston seems to think he will avoid prison if an alternative situation can be found." I thought back to my dreams. "At this point, I'm convinced Destiny has to have been the subject of my dreams. Assuming that is factual, I know that she spent time in the old mining camp near the shallow grave where we found the body of the man I'm sure she must have killed at some point in the past. I was looking through her eyes as she shared her memories with me, so I can't say that I got a good look at the young girl or the woman, but my sense was that Destiny and her family moved to the camp when she was a young girl. She was miserable about the move until she met a boy, who I assume was around her age, and they became friends." I frowned, "Or maybe they were already friends. I'm not sure, but I am sure that the image of this girl sitting on a wall waiting for the boy was a joyful memory. What I don't get is why she turned around and killed him years later."

"Are you sure it's the boy who was killed by the woman as an adult?" Wyatt asked.

"No. I'm not certain, but I do feel as if that is what occurred."

"Maybe this woman wants you to get the rest of the story. Maybe she wants you to understand why she did what she seems to have done."

I'd had that thought myself on more than one occasion, but by this point, I felt I actually had begun to understand the why. "I believe that Destiny killed the man she was waiting for out of a duty of some sort to her grandmother. I don't understand the details at this point, but she did say something in my dream about a son for a son." I pulled the medallion we'd found out of my pocket. I'd been carrying it around all week, hoping for inspiration. "We also found this on the man buried near the old camp cemetery. I think it might be important."

Wyatt accepted the medallion from me once I handed it to him. "It looks like something that a miner would wear. Maybe the emblem represents the mine on Grizzly Mountain." He flipped it over. "There's a word on the back."

"It translates to brother. Landon has done some digging on my behalf, and he seems to think that the medallion was utilized by a smaller group of miners with something in common. Like a union or a group of friends who worked together as a team."

"So everyone wouldn't have had the medallion, only those men who were part of this group or team."

I nodded. "That's what Landon thinks. He's still digging around for me. We're hoping that if a select group of men wore the medallion, determining who those men were and what they had in common might help us identify the man we found buried in the shallow grave near the cemetery. Not that identifying him will help us understand why this woman killed him, but it would provide a starting point for our research."

"Do you know if Landon scanned the medallion into the computer and did an image search for a match?" Wyatt asked.

"I'm not sure. Landon was working on it when we first got back, but then he had that work thing to take care of this week, and I haven't spoken to him since Tuesday morning."

"You know," Wyatt said, rubbing his thumb over the medallion's surface. "as long as you're going to be in Fairbanks, you might want to visit the mining museum. The volunteers working there are more knowledgeable than most about the specific mines and the towns that supported them that popped up in our area."

"That's actually a good idea. I think I'll try to stop by. Maybe I can even find someone who recognizes the medallion."

Chapter 14

Houston had to work longer than he had planned yesterday, so it was late by the time we made it to Fairbanks. His work seminar was scheduled to begin at eight o'clock the following morning, so we decided to have dinner at the hotel rather than dining out as we'd originally planned to do. Houston would be done with his seminar by five o'clock today and had promised that once he was finished with his work commitment, he'd be all mine until we headed home. I, for one, was looking forward to some couple time without either of our jobs, multiple animals, or emergency rescues to interrupt us.

Today, however, I was on my own. I'd originally planned on doing some shopping or sightseeing but decided that my first stop of the day would be to the mining museum Wyatt had suggested. I'd begun seriously considering the idea that I might not regain my power to connect until I figured out what the old woman in my dreams had been trying to share with me. I honestly felt that I had done everything I could, but perhaps there actually was more that needed to be done.

The museum was in a small building on a back street that didn't catch your eye unless you knew what you were looking for. Given the unimpressive exterior, I wasn't expecting much, which is why I was pleasantly surprised to find the interior of the building filled with literature, old photos, display cases with artifacts from the mines in the area, and even a few interactive exhibits that visitors could enjoy.

"Welcome," a man with fluffy white hair who looked to be in his seventies greeted. "Is this your first time here?"

"It is," I said.

The man smiled. "Excellent. My name is Chris. Feel free to look around, and if you have any questions, I'm here to answer what I can."

"Actually," I began, "I am here for a specific purpose." I pulled the medallion out of my pocket. "I wondered if you could tell me anything about this."

He took the piece of jewelry from me. "Where did you get this?"

"I bought it at a garage sale," I lied. I mean, I couldn't very well tell the man that I'd dug up a grave and then took the medallion from around the neck of the skeleton who wore it.

"This medallion was worn by a group of men who worked the mine on Grizzly Mountain. They all arrived at the mining camp around the same time and decided to form a collective of sorts. They referred to themselves as the brotherhood." He walked over to a bookshelf and took down a large book filled with hundreds of photos of the mine, the town, and the people who lived there. He turned to a page toward the middle of the book and pointed to a photo of six men, who all wore the medallion. "This photo was taken in nineteen thirty-two. A seventh man, Kent Kellerman, was part of the team who worked the mine in collaboration with the brotherhood. Kent died in a mining accident earlier in the year."

"Kent Kellerman," I said aloud. I remembered that the woman who'd been haunting my dreams was named Destiny Kellerman. "Do you know anything more about this man?"

He nodded. "A bit. My father was one of the seven members of the brotherhood, so I've taken some time to learn the history of the place."

"Your father was one of these men. Which one?"

He pointed to a young man with blond hair, dark eyes, and a huge smile.

"What was his name?"

"Gerald. He worked that mine until it closed in nineteen forty-six."

"And after the mine closed?" I asked.

"He moved to Anchorage for a while. He met my mother and decided to settle down. I was born in nineteen fifty. My father was already in his forties by then, so it turned out that I was an only child. My father truly loved my mother and me, but the love he held the closest to his heart was mining. He talked about his time up there at that mining town nonstop from the day I was old enough to listen until the day he died."

"So you know a lot of stories about the town."

Chris nodded. "I do. That town was unique in that it came after the gold rush that first started the migration to Alaska at the turn of the century. I don't think the mine on Grizzly Mountain made anyone rich, but there did seem to be enough gold up there to whet the appetites of the men who worked the vein."

"So, how did your father get involved with the mine and this group of men?" I wondered.

He pointed to a man standing near the center of the line of six men featured in the photograph. "This is Jeff Hanson. Jeff is the one who put the team together. When Jeff recruited my father, they were both living in Seattle. I'm not sure how Jeff knew about the mine. I guess he might have known someone who had gone on ahead. Anyway, Jeff was the sort to want to think things through and plan things out. He figured that if he showed up with a team, the chances of hitting it big would be increased. He recruited my father, who was still living with his parents at the time and ripe for some adventure, and I believe between him and my father, they recruited the other five men."

"So, did the seven original brotherhood members live in Seattle?" I wondered.

"I'm not sure if they all did, but I know that my father and Jeff lived there, as did a few others."

"Do you have any other photos of the men? At this point, I guess I'm the most interested in Kent, the man who isn't featured in the photo."

Chris continued to flip through the book that had taken someone a lot of time and effort to compile. He found the photo he was looking for. "This here is a photo of Kent with his family taken in nineteen thirty, which is the year the men headed to Alaska to chase what ended up being the tail end of the gold rush."

The man in the photo was handsome. He was standing next to a fragile-looking woman and a young girl who looked to be around six or seven if I had to guess.

"So, was Kent married when he came north?"

"He was."

"Do you know the names of the wife and daughter?" I asked.

"The wife was Grace, and the daughter was Destiny."

"Kent had a nice-looking family."

"That he did," the man agreed. "Unfortunately, that poor family was headed for tragedy from the moment they set foot on Grizzly Mountain."

"You mentioned that Kent died just before the photo of the six remaining men from the brotherhood was taken in nineteen thirty-two."

He nodded. "It was a terrible thing the way that young man died. Not only did the man suffer a slow death after being trapped by debris when the mine caved in, but there ended up being all sorts of controversy surrounding his death. Kent's poor wife couldn't take all the stress and grief that was brought about by her husband's horrific death and ended up killing herself."

"Oh no," I said. "That's awful. What happened to Destiny?"

"She was sent to live with her grandmother. I'm not sure what happened to her after that."

The man once again flipped through the book. "This here is a photo of Kent with Jeff. My father and Jeff were tight, but Kent and Jeff were like brothers. They grew up in the same area of Seattle, married around the same time, and had a child within months of the other."

I wondered if Jeff's child was the boy the girl sitting on the wall had been waiting for, assuming, of course, that Destiny had been remembering herself sitting on the wall, as I suspected had been the case.

"Do you know if Jeff kept in touch with Destiny after she left to live with her grandmother?" I asked.

"I don't know for sure if he had contact with the child, but I sort of doubt it. Kent's mother was an odd sort of woman. She was extremely prim and proper but also had this wild side. Some folks claimed that she was a witch. Now, keep in mind that I never met the woman, so everything I know about her I learned from others who liked to tell stories about the crazy old lady, but if the stories I heard as a child are even partially true, that woman had powers that we mere mortals wouldn't want to mess with."

"Powers?" I asked.

"As I said, there were those who thought that she was a witch. My father told me that Jeff told him that the old broad put a curse on him after her son died. My father laughed it off, but Jeff was actually somewhat concerned about it. The woman was crazy, and the death of her only child and her child's wife seemed to send her over the edge."

"If the woman was crazy, why did they send Destiny to live with her?"

He shrugged. "The woman was kin. That was the way things were done back then."

I guessed I could understand that. "So why did Kent's mother put a curse on Jeff? Was it because he was the one who talked her son into going to Alaska in the first place?"

"Partially, but I think it was mostly because the cave-in that killed Kent was Jeff's fault. He miscalculated, acted hastily, and set dynamite where it ought not to have been set."

"So Kent's mother thought that Jeff killed her son," I confirmed.

He shrugged. "That was the story I was told, but once again, I need to remind you that I wasn't even born until after the camp closed and everyone left. I can't say with any degree of certainty where truth ends and gossip begins."

"Is anyone still around who might have lived in the camp?"

He shrugged. "Not that I know of. It was a long time ago, and once the mine closed, the town turned into a ghost town overnight."

"So when exactly did Destiny go to live with her grandmother?" I asked.

"I believe it was within days of her mother's death. Her mother killed herself on New Year's Day in nineteen thirty-three, and Destiny was sent with a guide who was willing to see that she made it to Seattle."

If the woman I'd been connecting to was the same woman who had been sent to live with her crazy grandmother after her parents died, then I knew she eventually made it back to Alaska. I just wasn't sure when, and I wasn't sure why she had ended up living with her son in total isolation.

"Do you know what happened to Jeff after he left here?" I asked.

"He worked the mine until it closed, and then he headed to Montana. I heard that he bought some land and began raising cows. I don't know a lot about the details of his life after he left Alaska, but I did hear that he died as the result of a long illness in nineteen fifty-six."

"Just ten years after the mine closed."

He nodded.

If Jeff had died as the result of an illness, then he couldn't have been the one Destiny eventually killed and buried in the old cemetery on the mountain.

"You said Jeff and his wife had a child within months of Kent and his wife. Do you know if Jeff's child was a girl or boy?"

"Jeff and his wife had a son. They named him Collin."

"What about Collin? Do you know what happened to him?"

He shook his head. "No idea. My father didn't stay in contact with Jeff or his son after they moved. Toward the end, I think there was a lot of tension up there on that mountain, and folks who were once as close as brothers were barely talking to each other."

"I guess that makes sense. The mine must have stopped providing long before the decision was made to abandon it. Do you have a photo of Jeff's family?" I asked.

"I believe I do." He flipped through the book, stopping when he came to a page with a collage of photos. "This here is Jeff, his wife, Sophia, and his son, Collin. It was taken early on – before Kent died, and things began falling apart."

I looked at the son, and I knew. Destiny had killed Collin even though Collin hadn't been the one to kill her father. He had just been a child when the accident happened, as Destiny had been. I thought about my dreams and knew that the answer had to lie with the grandmother. Maybe she was a witch, as had been rumored. Maybe she actually had put a curse on Jeff once she realized he was the one who was responsible for her son's death. I remembered the vision of the young woman talking to the child. She had talked about a son for a son. Jeff had taken her son, so perhaps this woman had cursed his.

"I want to thank you for all the information you've provided. I do have one last question. The grandmother Destiny went to live with. It was Kent's mother. Right?"

"Yes. Destiny went to live with the old witch."

"Do you remember her name? The grandmothers, that is."

"Prudence. Prudence Kellerman."

Since I had a location, a first and last name, and an approximate date when Destiny went to live in Seattle with the woman, I supposed that Landon might be able to dig up something about the grandmother. I felt sure it had been Destiny who had been haunting my dreams, but perhaps in order to understand her, I needed to go back to her childhood before she returned to Alaska and killed the man her childhood friend had become.

I looked around the museum a bit longer and then decided to walk back toward the hotel. As I walked, I thought about my dreams, or at least what I remembered of them. The first dream I remembered having was the one in the cemetery. It was overgrown by this point, so the mine would have already closed, and the town would have been deserted. If the child had been sent to live with her grandmother in Seattle, then she must have returned years after the town was abandoned. I didn't know when exactly, but I felt sure it had to have been at least a decade after the last resident left.

If the skeleton in the graveyard that Houston and I found had been Collin Hanson, then it seemed to me that, as far as the world was concerned, he would have most likely been considered to be someone who had simply gone missing. If someone had realized what had happened to him, then chances were that someone would have recovered his body long before now.

I had to wonder where Bucky came into this. Had Destiny already had a son by the time she killed Collin, or did that come after. While I felt that I'd figured out a lot, there were still a lot of unanswered questions. Questions I wasn't sure could even be answered since everyone involved was dead.

If I never figured out what Destiny wanted me to know or find, would that mean my gift would simply disappear as suddenly as it had appeared? Not that I knew with any degree of certainty that the loss of my ability to connect was directly related to the dreams, but both events seemed to have originated around the same time.

Chapter 15

I bought a sandwich on my way back to the hotel. I figured I could eat it in the room while I worked on filling in a few of the blanks. I wasn't sure where Landon was today, but I knew that if I was actually going to get my answers, I'd need his techy know-how, so I figured that once I'd eaten, I'd call his cell phone. Before I did that, however, I wanted to call Serena to see how everything was going.

"It's going great," she answered once I'd called and asked. "You headed out so late yesterday that you had all the end-of-day walks and daily chores handled before you left, so all I needed to do was spend time with the animals. Wyatt came by after Neverland closed for the day, so we chatted and just hung out. He didn't have a shift until two this afternoon, so he took the dogs for their morning walk, and then I headed to work. Apparently, Landon will be by around dinner time to help me with the end-of-day walk and feedings, and then Wyatt plans to return when he gets off tonight to stay over."

"That was nice of both Landon and Wyatt."

"It really is nice of both men. I tried to tell Wyatt that he didn't need to be here while I slept, but he insisted that he felt better being there just in case. Besides, we really did have a nice time last night. We just sat and talked for hours. I've always thought of Wyatt as a somewhat less than serious sort, but he seems to have changed since the last time I spent any amount of time with him."

"Wyatt has changed. I think he's taken inventory of his life and has come to the decision that if he has certain goals and ambitions, he might want to start working on them."

"He certainly seems focused at this point."

I smiled. "He does, doesn't he? Did he tell you about the search-and-rescue dog he's getting?"

"Yes, he told me everything about the search-and-rescue dog he was getting the last time we pet-sat. This time, however, the trainer had just sent him lots of photos, which he seemed to be looking at obsessively. I asked him why he hadn't gotten a dog before this if he wanted one so badly, and his response was that he hadn't even been aware that he wanted one until Jake asked him about being Timber's handler. Now that he knows he has a dog on the way, he's super excited."

"Good for him. Wyatt is a nice guy. He'll make a good handler and a fun human for Timber, who is apparently still young enough to want lots of playtime."

"He does seem like a cool dog."

He did seem like a cool dog. I couldn't wait to meet him.

"So, how are things at the shelter today?" I asked, changing the subject.

"Slow. So far, we haven't had any drop-offs or adoption inquiries, but that's fine since it gives me time to work on my paperwork and the volunteers time to clean. By the way, have you worked out a date to release that bear cub we plan to return to his habitat?"

"I'm working with Fish and Game on the exact timing of the release, but it will be soon. Most likely, within the next few weeks. He's big enough and healthy enough to fend for himself. We've done a good job fattening him up, so we figured releasing him near hibernation time might be a good idea. He's been tagged and has a tracker, so if he doesn't do well on his own, we'll know about it, but personally, I think he's going to do fine."

"Okay, cool. That all sounds good. Someone just came in, so I need to go. Are you still planning to be home tomorrow?"

"I am. Most likely, sometime in the afternoon. I'll text you when I have a better time estimate."

With that, we both hung up.

After I hung up with Serena, I called Wyatt. If he'd been the one to take care of the morning walk and chores, then he'd be the one who would know if any of my animals was having an issue.

"Everyone's fine," he said after I'd called him and asked my question. "Denali is being a little standoffish, but that's typical of him. He was fine on the walk, but once we got home, he took up a position by the door, and it seems he intends to stay there. I warned Serena not to trip over him when she heads to your place after she gets off."

"I appreciate you helping out as much as you have."

"I'm happy to help out. Serena is an interesting woman. I've enjoyed getting to know her better. So, how is your trip going?"

I provided Wyatt with the highlights and then hung up and called Landon. If anyone could dig up additional information about Destiny, Collin, Jeff, and Kent, it would be Landon. Of course, I knew Jeff and Kent had died long before the details of everyone's life were displayed for all to see on the internet. I wasn't sure exactly when Collin had died, but I was willing to bet that it was long before the World Wide Web. Destiny had just recently died, but living an isolated life, as she seemed to have, made it unlikely that there would be much to discover about her either. Still, I knew that Landon would try, and you never knew when someone might have posted something about an ancestor that would help us begin to put together a more complete picture.

"Hey, Harm, what's up?" Landon asked when I called.

"I need a favor."

"For you, anything."

"My favor has to do with my visions, or more recently, lack of visions. I've learned a few things about the woman in my dreams, but I don't have a complete picture. I feel as if I need more."

"I have time. Why don't we set up a video chat so that if you have items to show me, you can just hold them up, and if I have items to share, I can do likewise."

"That sounds like a good plan. Let me set my computer up, and I'll call you right back."

Once my computer was set up and logged into the hotel Wi-Fi, I called Landon back. I started by going over everything I'd learned about Jeff, Kent, Collin, Destiny, and Prudence, and he responded by saying that he'd done a quick deep dive and found an online site that seemed to be based in Alaska. The site focused on the mining in the area, and, in addition to offering a lot of photos and historical facts, it also provided a platform for those with familial ties to share stories about their ancestors and the part they played in the short-lived gold rush. Given the fact that the height of gold fever in the area seemed to exist from the eighteen nineties through the first few years after the turn of the century, the mine on Grizzly Mountain was established and consequently shut down later than most of the mines in the area.

While the history surrounding the discovery of gold in the area was fascinating, the information I was actually interested in was the personal history of a handful of specific people.

"As you've already learned from others," Landon started in, "Kent Kellerman and Jeff Hanson were friends in Seattle. Both men were married with a child. Shortly after the mine on Grizzly Mountain opened, Jeff had the idea to pull up stakes in Seattle and head to Alaska, hoping to hit it rich. He convinced Kent to do the same, and the two men made the trip north, where they met up with the other five men who made up the brotherhood."

"So, did all these men know each other before arriving in Alaska?" I asked.

"Given the fact they seemed to band together early on, I believe so, although I haven't verified that fact at this point."

"Okay, so Kent and Jeff, plus five other men, created a cooperative and then moved to Alaska to work in the mine," I said. "I know that Kent and Jeff were good friends by this point, and based on what I've learned through my visions, their children, Destiny and Collin, became good friends as well. I also know that Kent eventually lost his life due to a mining accident that seems to have been Jeff's fault. I know that Kent's wife was unable to deal with things, and on January first of the following year, she killed herself, and Destiny was sent to live with Kent's mother. It appears, based on my visions, that Kent's mother, Prudence, was pretty crazy herself and managed to convince Destiny that it was her duty to kill Jeff's son as an act of vengeance for the death of her son. Based on my visions, it appears she did that at some later point. But I don't understand what this has to do with me and my gift. I feel like I've been able to figure out quite a lot, yet I still can't connect. I can feel the hole where my psychic ability once lived."

"Maybe you just need to give it time," Landon counseled.

"Maybe, but I'm not used to this total silence in my head. I feel as if the loss of my gift is linked to this woman. To this point, I figured that once I did whatever she needed me to do, my gift would return, but I found the body she seemed to have wanted me to find, and I got the story. I'm not sure what more I can do."

Landon didn't answer right away. I assumed he was considering the situation.

"I assume that the family never knew what had become of Collin," he eventually said. "Maybe you need to find his family and give them closure."

"That sounds reasonable to me. Can you do that? Find his family."

"Perhaps. I have enough information to give me a starting place. I know the name of the victim, his mother's name, and the town of primary residence. It might take me a while since all this occurred quite a while ago, but I'll start working on it as soon as we hang up. Is there anything else I should be looking for?"

I thought about this before answering. "I don't know. I need to think about what this woman might have wanted from me. Maybe contacting any family Collin might have left in the world will be enough. Although…" I said.

"Although?"

"The woman was worried about her son. I guess I'll have Houston reach out to the police in the area where the woman and her son lived. Hopefully, they've found a way to take care of him that doesn't include jail time. Neither Dani nor Jordan pressed charges in relation to their captivity, so it seemed like they were going to try to find a good option for the guy."

"Are you sure that the loss of your powers is associated with this woman and some sort of task you still need to perform?"

"No, I'm not sure at all. I settled on that because it's the only new thing in my life since I realized I'd lost my ability to connect."

"You said the last time you remember having your powers was when we were looking for the man who kidnapped those kids. That was almost two months ago. The dreams you've been having have only been going on for a month or so. Were you able to connect between arriving home from the fiasco with the missing kids and the first dream?"

I slowly shook my head. "I didn't need to connect, so I didn't try. If something other than my connection with this woman is responsible, I can't imagine what it might be."

"Your gift did come on all of a sudden."

I frowned. "So, do you think my ability to connect left as abruptly as it began?"

"I think that's a possibility. You were in intense pain when the gift first manifested itself. Val was lost in the storm, and you had all but given up hope of finding her. You wanted to talk to her one last time so badly. You wanted Val to know you loved her and were there for her in her last moments. It was your need to connect, to find comfort in a moment of intense pain that seemed to have created a psychic connection in the first place."

"So what are you saying?" I asked, staring into my computer monitor in an attempt to look him in the eye despite the distance between us.

"I don't know what I'm saying. It's just that if intense pain caused the situation in the first place, maybe intense happiness is the catalyst that sends it away."

I knew exactly what Landon was getting at. My gift came to me during the lowest time in my life. Val was missing, and it looked unlikely that we'd find her. I was deeply traumatized when I realized that I'd never see her again, nor would I ever have the chance to tell her everything that was in my heart. In the moment when my pain and desperation became unbearable, she was suddenly there in my head. While I was happy to have been given the chance to connect with her one last time, her death hit me hard. I knew deep down that I'd never really be happy again. And I hadn't been. Not that I walked around in a state of misery all the time, but my loss was always with me, so I guess it was true that I'd never really experienced complete joy since Val's death.

"Houston," I said.

Landon shrugged. "It's a theory."

Chapter 16

Could Landon be right? Could the fact that Houston finally committed to me and to Alaska and thereby ended my torment over his likely departure have been the catalyst that finally broke the state of deeply buried sorrow I'd been living with since I'd lost Val? I did have to admit that I'd been happier in the past couple of months than I'd been for a very long time. Not that I'd lived my life in misery since Val had died. Jake and the entire search-and-rescue team had been great, and most days of the week, I found myself in a state of being that most would describe as happiness. But it was also true that the happiness I'd felt had been twinged with loss and sorrow before Houston and I had moved our relationship to the next level.

I was sure I was in love with Houston, and now that he'd managed to work through his issues, I felt like we could finally be together. I was happy. He seemed happy. Everything should be wonderful, and it was. But if my happiness robbed me of the one thing that seemed to give my life true meaning, could I honestly let it go?

Maybe I was creating a problem where one didn't actually exist. Landon had made an offhand comment about the change in status of the relationship that Houston and I had been working on for years, and Landon's comment made sense, but that didn't necessarily mean that he was right. I had been sure that the loss of my ability to connect with others in pain had been a direct result of my psychic connection to Destiny, and at this moment, unless new information was obtained that would confirm that fact, that hadn't actually seemed to be the case.

I sat on the edge of the bed and thought of the faces of the people I'd been able to save or simply comfort by entering their mental space during the darkest moments of their lives. I knew that my gift, while hard on me at times, had made all the difference to them. And then I thought of Houston's face and his gentle and encouraging smile. The way his mouth turned up just a little when he first noticed me walk into a room and the strong presence he brought to my life when I was feeling weak. Both the gift I brought to the world and the gift Houston brought to my life were so important to me. Surely, fate wouldn't insist that I must choose.

After coming to the realization that sitting here, dwelling on what might never come to be, was pointless, I decided to go for a walk. Houston wouldn't be back from his seminar for another two hours, and I knew that if I sat here wallowing in self-pity while I waited, I'd be a nervous wreck by the time he finally arrived.

The section of town featuring cute little mom-and-pop shops was only a few blocks from the hotel, so I headed in that direction. I wasn't sure if I was actually in the mood to buy anything, but walking up and down the street looking in the windows seemed a lot more satisfying than anything else I'd come up with. Some shops carried outerwear, shops that sold candy and other snacks, shops that sold local crafts, and shops that sold tourist items such as t-shirts, coffee mugs, and even socks featuring the Alaska logo. I had always found these novelty items fun to look at, but today, I found myself drawn to a secondhand bookstore that didn't look new but had never called out to me before.

I wasn't much of a reader, but when the sign in the doorway was turned from closed to open right in front of my eyes, I decided to head inside.

"Can I help you find anything?" the friendly-looking woman asked after I entered the store.

"No, thank you. I'm just window shopping while I wait for a friend, but I'd like to look around if that's okay."

"That's fine. I wasn't even going to be open today, but my dental appointment didn't take as long as I thought I would, so I decided to open up for a couple hours so those who had books on hold could come in and pick them up." She nodded toward a table at the front of the shop. "I recently added a few new releases to my used book inventory if you're interested in something from the top ten bestseller list. I enjoy the feel and musky smell of the older books, but many customers want to see what their favorite author or celebrity is up to."

I thanked the woman and headed toward the back of the store where some of the oldest hardbound novels had been shelved. Most of the shelves in this part of the store were covered with dust, and, as evidenced by the lack of scrape marks on the shelves made by books that were slid in and out along the dusty shelves, it appeared that many of the books on display had been sitting in the same place they were displayed now for years and possibly decades.

Pulling a book bound with a genuine leather cover toward me, I considered the title. *The Esoteric Constraints of Our Inner Lives and the Unique Individuals Who Can Experience and Understand Them.*

Okay, that was a mouthful, but it resonated with me for some unknown reason.

Esoteric constraints of our inner lives? I guess that referred to limitations due to the inability of those in the general population to easily understand what was going on in our inner lives. In most cases, the experiences we had and thoughts we didn't verbalize were ours alone to experience. Of course, a few individuals could experience the inner lives of others, at least to a degree.

Making a decision, I purchased the book and then returned to the hotel. I wasn't sure at this point that the book had been put in my path by some divine design, but it seemed to fit what I was going through, and I figured it couldn't hurt to take a look and see what the author had to say about such things.

Later, though, because right now, I needed to get ready for my night out with Houston. I'd brought a fun sweater I'd been looking for a reason to wear.

"You look nice," Houston said after kissing me hello once he returned to the hotel.

"Thank you. I bought this sweater years ago but haven't had the opportunity to wear it until now. How was your seminar?"

He smiled. "It went well. I think my talk was well received, and I learned a lot from the talks and discussions hosted by others. Did you have a nice day sightseeing?"

"I did." I decided to fill him in on the information I'd picked up about Destiny and the role she played in what seems to have been a drama with deeply seated roots but left out the part about where our newly found love was possibly the reason I was no longer able to help those who desperately needed someone to hear them. "I met a man at the mining museum who had a lot of helpful information to share. I figured I could catch you up over dinner."

Houston began to unbutton his shirt. "Let me wash up a bit, and then we'll go. I made us a reservation at a steakhouse on the river one of the men who attended the seminar told me about."

"That sounds good," I said as Houston wandered into the bathroom to brush his teeth.

"I guess the place is known for steak and seafood, but they also have pasta dishes and other types of protein," he called toward me as he squeezed toothpaste onto his brush.

I loved these ordinary moments. Simple moments when the normalcy of the task at hand seemed to cement the idea that Houston and I were a real couple in my mind. We'd been "just friends" for so long, and at the time, I was mostly okay with that, but now that I'd enjoyed the intimacy of chatting through an open bathroom door while Houston washed up or shaved, I sincerely doubted that we could ever go back to being "just friends" the way we had been.

"I'd been thinking that dinner at a steakhouse might be nice earlier today. I didn't bring a dress. Do you think what I have on will be okay?" I called back, although he was in full brush mode and couldn't reply by this point.

Houston spit and rinsed before answering. "I was told that the place is casual. They have an outdoor deck, and it sounded like customers show up in shorts and t-shirts in the summer. The officer who told me about the place did mention that their indoor dining is a bit less casual, but he also reminded me that this is still Alaska, so jeans and a sweater are fine."

In addition to my new sweater, I'd put dressy black denim pants on, so I figured I was okay.

As promised, the steak house was lovely. Huge windows overlooking the river dominated one wall that looked out over a seasonal deck, which was closed for the winter but must be breathtaking in the summer. The hostess sat us near the river rock fireplace, which was fine since it was completely dark outside, so even if we'd been seated near a window, there wouldn't have been anything to see.

"Everything looks good," I said as we studied the menu.

"I was going to have a filet, but I think I might try the crab and lobster special," Houston responded.

"That sounds good to me as well. I think I'll have the crab and lobster special as well." I folded my menu and set it on the edge of the table, where the waiter could easily retrieve it.

Once we'd ordered, I filled Houston in on my conversation with the man at the museum.

I could see his frown deepening as he seemed to be processing everything. Eventually, he spoke. "Okay, so let me see if I have this right. The woman who was invading your dreams before her death is a miner's daughter named Destiny Kellerman."

I nodded.

He continued. "Destiny first came to Alaska with her father, Kent Kellerman, and mother, Grace. During their time at the mining camp on Grizzly Mountain, Kent was killed in a mining accident that seems to have been the result of a mistake made by Kent's best friend, Jeff Hanson."

Again, I nodded.

He took a sip of his wine and then continued. "Grace was so distraught over her husband's death that she took her own life, leaving her daughter, who we think was somewhere around ten years old, alone. The daughter, Destiny, was sent to live with Kent's mother, Prudence."

"So far, so good," I said.

"Prudence, a resident of Seattle, was some sort of crazy woman who wanted vengeance for the death of her only son, but instead of killing Jeff, whom she seems to have blamed, she cursed him. The curse demanded the life of his son as retribution for the loss of her son."

"Basically."

Houston's frown deepened. "But Prudence didn't plan to use her own hand to take the life of the son. She planned for her granddaughter, Destiny, to do the deed at some future time."

Again, I nodded.

"You realize this entire story is crazy."

"Yes, I do realize that. And if I hadn't lived it in my dream state and knew it was true, I would have thought the whole thing to be just a crazy legend without any roots in reality. Destiny was a child when her father was killed, and she was sent to live with her grandmother. She was likely still at an age when she was easily molded by the older woman who seems to have had a strong and demanding personality."

"But Destiny didn't kill the son of the man who her grandmother blamed for the death of her own son until much later," Houston pointed out.

"That much seems to be true. I can't say how old Destiny was when she finally killed the man the boy had become, but based on the condition of the cemetery in my dream, I'm going to say she was thirty or maybe even older when she finally killed Collin. That seems like a long time to wait. She must have had a reason to do so. In the dream, it seemed that the time and place were predestined. It felt like she hadn't had control over any of it."

"How can that be?" Houston asked.

I shrugged. "Maybe Prudence really was a witch, and maybe she actually did put a curse on Jeff and his son. Maybe the people involved were simply pawns in her crazy need for vengeance."

Houston sat quietly for a moment. I knew this was a lot to swallow, especially if you weren't starting from a position of believing that curses were real.

"So Destiny did her duty, and then she took her son and went to live out her life in isolation."

I shrugged once again. "I guess that is how things worked out, but I'm unclear at this point as to the timeline of the whole thing. I'm not even sure if Bucky had been around when Destiny killed Collin or if he was born at some point after that event. As for why she moved herself and her son to such an isolated place, I think she simply couldn't live with what she had done, so she basically hunkered in to live her life well away from people in general."

The waiter brought our salads, so the conversation paused while we ate. The salad was good. Fresh greens topped with plump shrimp and chunks of goat cheese. The dressing had been listed on the menu as "house dressing," so I wasn't sure what to expect, but whatever was drizzled atop the greens was very good. It had a creamy look and feel but was thin rather than thick like most creamy dressings tended to be. If the rest of the meal was as good as the salad, then I suspected we were in for a treat.

Once we'd finished our salads, I decided to change the subject, so I asked about Houston's plans for the upcoming week.

"The week ahead should be fairly typical as long as nothing unexpected comes up. Kojak has an appointment with Kelly," he referred to the local veterinarian, "so I think I'll have her x-ray his front right shoulder as long as he's there."

"Is he still limping?"

"Off and on. It seems better now, but since it's been an issue since this past summer, I figured that I'd have it looked at as long as we were in the office."

My cell phone dinged, which had me looking toward my shoulder bag. "I'm sorry. I meant to turn it off." I opened the bag and took my cell phone out to turn it off when I noticed the text from Jake. They had an ongoing rescue that wasn't going well, and he hoped I might be able to connect with the subject of the rescue from where I was. I texted him back and reminded him that it didn't work that way. I didn't even need to go into the whole "my gift is still on the fritz" thing since, as a general rule, I needed to have some degree of proximity to the victim or involvement in the rescue to make a connection even when things were working the way they were supposed to.

"Is everything okay?" Houston asked.

"No, not really. Jake and the team are involved in a rescue that isn't going well, and he hoped I could try to connect with the missing person, but it doesn't work that way. It's not as if I can connect with anyone at any time. I need to have some degree of proximity."

He raised a brow. "I've seen you connect from distances further than we are from Rescue."

I guessed he had me there. "You're right, I have, but in those cases, I was meant to help those individuals. It was as if they reached out with a silent hope or prayer that I was able to intercept." I looked around. "I can't lay down here and try to connect."

"If it's important, I'll explain to the server that something came up and that we can't stay and finish our meal. I'll ask our server to put the food in to-go boxes. Our room has a microwave, so we can reheat it."

I hesitated. I wanted to help if I could, but I didn't want to try and fail, which, at this point, was pretty much what I suspected would happen. Doing so would only bring my problem to the forefront of everyone's attention. Still, if there was any chance at all…

"Okay," I finally said. "Give me the truck keys, and I'll head out where it's quiet. Meanwhile, you can see to the food."

I told Jake what I was doing and headed out to the truck. I asked him to send photos of the missing person or persons, and then I asked him to fill me in on the details.

"Two families with six children between them rented a house on the lake," Jake began. "Three of the older children, aged nine through eleven, decided to head down to the water to skip rocks. The three children made it back to the house just fine, but after they returned, everyone realized that the youngest of the six, a four-year-old boy named Eli, was missing. According to the oldest boy, an eleven-year-old named Timothy, Eli had wanted to go with the older kids when they left to head down to the lake, but the older kids didn't want him tagging along, so they told him that he couldn't go with them. Eli's parents believe that Eli may have decided to follow the older children even though they told him to stay home. If that was the case, it seemed like Eli lost track of the others at some point. The parents had been unsuccessfully looking for the boy, so they called Houston's office. Jacob is on call today and has been trying to help locate the child, but he decided early on to call me, so we have been helping out almost since the beginning. So far, the boy still hasn't been found. Now that the sun has set, time is of the essence."

"Why didn't you call me sooner?" I asked.

"I knew you were looking forward to some time away, and it has seemed like you've needed a break. To be honest, in the beginning, Sitka and Yukon were both alerting regularly, so I figured we'd find the boy sooner rather than later. Of course, I had no way of knowing that while the dogs seemed to be onto something at first, they would end up walking in circles. I need you to try, Harm."

I reminded Jake that I hadn't been able to connect for the past couple of months, but I agreed to try. I settled into the seat and got as comfortable as I could. I focused on the image of the boy in the photo Jake had texted me. Houston showed up with the food by the time I'd been at it about fifteen minutes. We agreed that we should head back to the hotel, and I kept trying to connect while we made the trip back toward town.

As I had predicted would be the case, while I did try to connect with Eli and wanted with all my heart to find him before it was too late, I ended up having zero luck. After some discussion, Houston and I decided to eat our reheated meals and head home, even though we weren't scheduled to check out until the following day. If there was an active rescue, I needed to be there whether I had my powers to connect or not. Houston felt the same way even though Jacob assured him he had things covered.

Chapter 17

By the time we arrived in Rescue, Jake had figured out that Eli had been hiding in a drainage pipe that fed into the lake from the road above. The reason that the dogs had been walking in circles was because they were able to pick Eli's scent up at both open ends of the pipe. The pipe somehow prevented them from making the connection between the two openings. In the end, Eli was cold and scared but unharmed. As had been theorized, Eli had followed the older children when they'd taken off for the lake but had become disoriented once he'd lost sight of them. I was happy that Eli was found unharmed, yet concerned that I hadn't connected with the boy. Given the level of fear he'd been feeling, combined with the natural inclination for children so young to let me in, I should have been able to reach out and offer comfort.

"Is everything okay?" Houston asked me the following day.

"Everything is fine. I realize we talked about going hiking this afternoon, but Landon called to let me know that he found some information about Collin's family and asked about coming by this afternoon."

"That's fine. We'll walk the dogs to the lake and back and then make breakfast. I noticed you only have a couple of eggs, but you have milk and bread, so I figured I'd make my famous French toast."

"That sounds good. I also have some bacon that we can fry to go with the French toast."

Houston began layering his warm outerwear on in preparation for our walk. "Did Landon mention what he found out?" he asked as he helped me with my parka. Once we were both bundled up, he opened the cabin door to allow us all to exit.

"Not really. I originally asked Landon to find a family member who might want to offer an opinion about what should be done with Collin's remains once the spring thaw allows us to relocate him should we decide that's the best course of action. There's been a lot of snow on the mountain since we first uncovered the body, so moving him this winter is probably no longer an option."

"If nothing else, I guess you can pass the medallion along to whoever is determined to be the next of kin. I can't help but wonder how Collin even ended up with it. He was only a child when the seven original men banded together."

I whistled to Denali to hold up a bit. He seemed to be extra energetic this morning. "I suppose the medallion we found might have belonged to Collin's father, Jeff. We don't know what became of Collin after Destiny left the area, at least not until she killed him years later."

"It sounds as if Jeff had passed away by the time his son was killed, so it stands to reason that Jeff left the medallion to his son. Of course," Houston added, "if Jeff died of natural causes before Destiny killed Collin, then killing Collin wouldn't have affected Jeff at all."

I supposed that Houston had a point. If Prudence actually had been a witch, and if the timing of Collin's death by Destiny's hand had been predestined, then it seemed as if the witch would have timed things to ensure the maximum impact on the life of the man she was trying to punish in the first place.

"I know the legend states that Prudence was a witch and that it was her curse that set what was to come in motion, but I'm not sure I believe in witches," Houston said.

"And curses?" I asked.

He shrugged. "If there are no witches, then I suppose there can be no curses."

I wasn't sure I agreed, but I decided not to say as much. Before discovering my ability to psychically connect with others, I didn't believe in anything magical, but now that I'd experienced it personally, I had to admit that if psychic abilities were real, then perhaps the rest of it was as well.

"It looks as if your cougar is still in the area," Houston said, pointing at huge paw prints in the mud.

"It looks like he is. We'll need to keep our eyes open and the dogs close. I think I told you I came around the corner a while back and ended up face-to-face with a grizzly."

"I'm surprised the dogs didn't sense him long before you noticed him on the trail."

I frowned. "Yeah, that is odd. That was the first time I'd seen that particular bear in the area, and I'm hopeful he was just passing through."

Houston's second in command called just as we reached the lake. We planned to allow the younger dogs to run and the older dogs to rest, so he went ahead and took it. After he hung up, he informed me that a couple of the stores in town had been broken into during the overnight hours. Since we'd returned from Fairbanks early, he thought he'd go in and look into the situation once we'd returned from our walk. I was meeting with Landon, so that was fine with me. If we had vandals in the area, it seemed like a good idea to nip things in the bud sooner than later.

"Hey, Landon," I greeted one of my best friends a few hours later. "Come on in. Would you like something to drink?"

"No, I'm fine."

I motioned for him to have a seat. "So what did you find?"

Landon responded to my question. "I was able to track down a man named Gavin Fisher, who, as it turns out, is the great-grandson of Collin's younger sister, Gwen. According to Gavin, Collin never married or had children, but Gavin informed me that Gwen had had four children, twelve grandchildren, and twenty-six great-grandchildren. According to Gavin, while he had never met Collin, he had been led to believe that the man and his parents had moved back to Seattle immediately after the mine closed but had returned to Alaska at some point, never to be seen or heard from again. The family had always wondered what had become of the man, who, to Gavin's knowledge, had never settled down. Gavin seemed happy to have answers and promised to fill in other family members who might be old enough to remember who Collin had been."

I supposed that my task was complete with the discovery of Gavin.

"Did Gavin have an opinion about what should happen to Collin's remains?" I asked.

"It was Gavin's opinion that Collin should remain where Destiny had left him. He'd been there all this time, and Gavin saw no point in moving him at this point."

"And the medallion?" I asked.

"He gave me an address to mail it to."

"I guess that means this case is wrapped up."

"I guess it is. Still no powers?" Lansdon asked, knowing full well that as of last night, my powers hadn't returned since he had been part of the rescue.

"Still no powers," I confirmed. "I talked to Houston about Bucky, and he planned to look into that situation, but it's his understanding that the guy who provides law enforcement for the village closest to where Destiny and Bucky lived is aware of his situation and is taking responsibility for finding Bucky a comfortable living situation. If my powers don't return soon, I suppose I'll have no choice but to conclude that the loss of my ability never was related to my connection with Destiny as I thought it had been."

"Houston?" he asked.

"No," I said in a tone that was louder than was warranted. I knew what Landon was really asking, and there was no way I was willing to go there.

I didn't elaborate, and Landon seemed to let it go, so when I asked about the research he'd been conducting for his job, he went into more detail than might have otherwise been warranted. I appreciated that Landon had elected not to pursue his line of reasoning that my relationship with Houston could be behind the change in my ability to connect because when it came right down to it, I didn't have an argument against such a theory that was likely to stand the test of time. I mean, as I'd already reminded myself multiple times, it had been intense emotion that had brought my ability into my life in the first place.

"What do you think about the Wyatt and Serena thing?" Landon asked once he'd exhausted the subject of his work project.

"There's a Wyatt and Serena thing?"

He shrugged. "Neither have said as much exactly, but I stopped by yesterday to see if they needed any help with the animals, and there was definitely a vibe between the two."

Serena had professed her love for Harley on more than one occasion, but even she had to see that it was unlikely that her infatuation was ever going to lead to anything. Maybe she'd finally given up on the Hollywood Hero and settled for the Hometown Hunk.

"I guess they have spent lots of time together the past couple of weeks," I admitted. "Wyatt is a sweet guy, and there's no doubt he's very good-looking in a flirty boy-next-door sort of way. And Serena is one of the sweetest and most caring people I know. They both like to have fun and seem to have a soft spot for animals." I paused to think this over. "I know that Wyatt has been a real player in the past, and Serena has seemed to be totally committed to the idea of a relationship with Harley, but they actually would be good together."

"I wouldn't be marrying them off just yet." Landon laughed. "The only thing I know is that I picked up a vibe. But I agree that Wyatt has matured a lot in the past year. He seems to have focused his energy and, as a result, seems to have left the serial dating behind. He bought a house, is getting a dog, and he's even taking classes online."

I raised a brow. "Wyatt's taking online classes? He hasn't mentioned taking classes to me."

"He decided he wanted to be an EMT. He already has the skills with his experience with search-and-rescue, but he needs to pass a test for certification, so he's getting the knowledge he needs."

"Good for him," I said. "I can't believe he never mentioned it. We both work at Neverland, so we talk almost every day."

"I think he's keeping it quiet for now. In fact, I probably shouldn't have mentioned it, so maybe you can wait to talk to him about it until he brings it up."

"I will," I promised. "And maybe you can keep the struggle I'm experiencing with my gift to yourself for now. I realize that if we have another rescue, and I'm still unable to connect, the others will begin to wonder, but I don't want to bring the theory about Houston into things if I don't have to."

"Are you afraid that you'll be put in a position of having to choose?" he asked.

"I am," I admitted. "But I guess I'm even more worried that Houston will choose for me. If he thinks our relationship might cost someone their life who would otherwise have been saved, then I suspect he'll take matters into his own hands by walking away from the relationship before we even get started."

"Maybe the gift, or as you often referred to it, curse, was never supposed to last beyond a certain point."

I tilted my head a bit. "Do you think my ability had a shelf life that would have played itself out regardless of anything that was happening in my life?"

He shrugged. "Maybe. I obviously can't know that with any degree of certainty, but since we're looking at all the possible explanations, I think a natural end to an unnatural state of being should be considered."

I supposed the idea that my gift had come in a limited supply all along was a possibility. I didn't necessarily think it was the most likely theory, but it was a theory I liked much better than the theory of my relationship with Houston being at the bottom of things.

"There doesn't seem to be any way to know what's going on," I said. "I mean, if you stop to think about it, without information we don't have and likely have no way of getting, I may never know. I could upend my life and start trying things that may or may not work, but that seems reckless without further information."

"I agree. It's true that you can't know why your visions seem to have ended at this point. You could break up with Houston, causing you both a lot of pain, only to find that nothing changed."

"Exactly," I said, agreeing with the first thing Landon had said about the subject. "It's probably best to wait and see what happens rather than jumping in with a bunch of changes."

"I agree."

"Okay, then. That's what I'm going to do," I decided. "But as I said, it might be best to keep this whole thing between the two of us for now."

"Agreed."

I reached out and gave Landon a long hug. He was such a good friend. I wasn't sure what I'd do without him. I knew there had been a time when he'd had a little crush on me, but I hadn't shared those feelings, so I hadn't encouraged his attention, and he eventually seemed to have adjusted his expectations so we could maintain our friendship status.

"Thanks again for helping me wrap things up with Destiny and for coming by to help me talk through the other," I said.

"Any time."

"You really are a good friend."

He nodded and smiled, but I noticed that his smile didn't quite reach his eyes.

Chapter 18

"The warehouse looks so good," I said weeks later as Harley showed me around the massive building he'd rented for the Halloween fundraiser for the shelter. "I love the decorations. The stage looks like it's always been there."

"My set crew did do a good job."

"Set crew?" I asked. "As in professional set crew?"

He nodded. "I figured I could get a few of my guys to volunteer their time in exchange for a free vacation, so I made the offer. Ava being here has given the event authenticity in the eyes of the Hollywood gang. I actually think this might be our best fundraiser yet."

"Wow. I'm excited to see how the movie slash live-action sing-along works out. Serena and Wyatt signed up for bit parts, and according to them, we are all in for a real treat."

Harley smiled. "I think so. All the locals who volunteered have done a wonderful job learning their parts. I've even decided to film the event and show it to my Hollywood friends during a future party."

I reached out and gave Harley a hug. "Thank you again for everything you've done for the shelter. I know I've thanked you at least a million times in the past, but I never want you to think we're taking advantage of you and your superstar status."

"You aren't taking advantage of me," he assured me. "I live here the same as you and consider the shelter my personal project, the same as you. There are times when I feel like I should be thanking you for all you do."

I laughed. "Okay, we'll thank each other and then let it drop. Are you still coming by Neverland for dinner?"

"I am. I'll be bringing a few friends with me. Maybe you can reserve that eight-top near the window."

"I will. By friends, do you mean guests from LA?"

He nodded. "All of a sudden, Rescue, Alaska is the 'in' place to vacation. Of course, I suppose the real draw might be the free room and board my guest rooms provide."

"Well, I'm anxious to meet your friends."

"And they're excited to meet you as well."

I paused to inhale deeply once Harley and I left the temporary theater. I loved this time of the year. We'd had a few small snowstorms, but nothing severe enough to cause any problems. Things in town and at the shelter had slowed to the point that Neverland was only open on weekends. This gave Houston and me a lot more time together. Time that I felt we needed to cement our relationship. My gift still hadn't returned, and the idea that the reason it hadn't returned was due to the level of complete happiness and contentment that Houston brought to my life did linger, but since I realized that there was no way I could ever choose, I decided to stick to my decision to simply wait and see what happened. So far, there hadn't been any rescues the dogs couldn't handle. If the life of an innocent person came down to the gift I'd once had, I supposed I might need to decide, but for now, a decision wasn't required, so the best course of action seemed to be to do nothing.

"Is everything okay?" Harley asked.

I nodded. "I guess I just got lost in my thoughts, but everything is fine. Better than fine. Everything is great."

He took my hand in his and walked me toward his truck. "I guess I should realize by now that you tend to simply float away at times. You were like that even when we were kids."

I turned my head to look directly at him. "Was I?"

"You were. Not always, of course, but sometimes. You have always been a deep thinker. I guess you simply get lost in your thoughts at times."

"I guess," I agreed. "So, is there anything I should know about your LA friends?"

"Know?"

"You know. Is anyone allergic to shellfish, or is anyone currently in a relationship with you that can be labeled as anything other than friendship?"

He smiled. "You want to know if I'm currently dating any of my guests, don't you?"

I shrugged.

"No, I am not currently dating any of my guests."

"Not currently dating?" I asked.

"There is one woman in the group I dated in the past. Lisa. But it was nothing serious. Just someone to help me pass the time while I wait."

"Wait for what?"

He just smiled.

I rolled my eyes and changed the subject. "I guess you must be relieved that Serena and Wyatt have started dating."

"I am glad. I love Serena like a sister and appreciate everything she has done for the community and the shelter, but we would never work as anything other than friends. I used to feel like I was walking a delicate line with her, but now that she has Wyatt and the two seem to be hitting it off, I feel like I can relax a bit."

"I figured that Wyatt would make things less awkward between you and Serena. I'm happy they found each other. They really do seem happy."

"They do," he agreed as he started his truck and headed back toward his house, where I had left my Jeep. "Should we take the dogs down to the river? It's at its lowest point right about now, and Brando loves running around in it."

"That sounds good. We'll stop and pick my Jeep up, and then you can follow me home."

"What time do you need to be at Neverland?"

"Not until four. We have plenty of time to walk the dogs before I need to start getting ready. You can tell me about your next movie while we walk. I heard this one is supposed to be different from any you have done in the past."

"It is different. There's still a lot of action, but this one is actually a love story."

"Really? A love story. What sort of a love story?"

"Boy falls in love with girl. Circumstances separate them. Then years later, they meet up again."

"Sounds predictable."

He winked. "Not as predictable as you might think."

USA Today best-selling author Kathi Daley lives in beautiful Lake Tahoe with her husband, Ken. When she isn't writing, she likes spending time hiking the miles of desolate trails surrounding her home. Find out more about her books at www.kathidaley.com

Printed in Great Britain
by Amazon